HORROR HOUSE OF PERVERSION

CARL JOHN LEE

SPOILER-FREE CONTENT WARNINGS

I know, it might seem crazy to some of you to have content warnings in an extreme horror book, but some folk out there like to enjoy their brutality without being reminded of a certain traumatic event from their past, so deal with it.

This book contains —
violence
sex
child death (implied)
rape/sexual assault
homophobic & misogynistic language

For Roger

PART I

Remember That Time?

1

NEVER PICK UP A HITCHHIKER.

That's what Cal's mother had always told him.

You never know who you're going to get, she used to say, and he always laughed because it reminded him of that dumb Tom Hanks movie.

Picking up a hitchhiker is like a box of chocolates. You never know if you're gonna get a psycho, or a rapist, or a murderer, or a—

Ah, his mom was full of shit. He had heard the stories growing up, the urban legends about the man with the razor blade concealed in his mouth, or the ghostly figure who vanishes from the car.

"Stupid bitch," he muttered as he pulled over onto the side of the empty forest road to pick up the lone hitchhiker. Rain thrummed on the roof of his Mercedes, and he glanced in the rearview, watching the girl as she unhurriedly stalked towards the vehicle. He leaned over to the passenger door and threw it open.

"Get in," he shouted, unsure if she could hear him over the torrential downpour.

She was in no rush. Her clothes were plastered to her body, the white skirt sticking to her pale legs like translucent skin, moonlight reflecting off the slick surface of her black jacket. What the hell was she doing out here in the middle of nowhere? And in this weather?

He pictured his mom wagging an admonishing finger at him from the other side of the country.

"Sorry, mom," he smiled, then forced her image out of his mind. He had more important matters at hand. He glanced at himself in the mirror, brushing his hair with his hand. Then he drew his lips back in a grimace, inspecting his teeth. Not bad, nothing stuck between them. He was looking good. Did he smell good? He hadn't farted for a while, so that was something. Still, the open door would clear out any unwanted odors. The girl finally reached the car and got in. Her drenched skirt had turned see-through, and Cal noticed with a grin that her white panties were visible through the sodden material.

"Hell of a day, huh?" he said.

She slammed the door shut, cutting off the rain. He normally hated when people slammed the door. Cal treated his car better than he treated most people. The girl settled herself in the passenger seat, staring straight ahead, not acknowledging him. Though her wet hair obscured much of her face, he could tell she was pretty. Real pretty, with full lips and soft features. Young, too. She couldn't be older than twenty.

She's less than half your age, he thought.

The idea turned him on.

"So, where are you going?"

The girl stared ahead. "I don't care," she said. "Just drive."

Cal nodded. "Anything you say, baby. You mind if I call you baby?"

She turned away from him, staring out the passenger window. Cal drove on. The sun had disappeared behind the trees, the sky darkening. Soon night would fall. He had been on the road for sixteen hours, and he was tired. He would need to rest soon. Another ten-hour journey awaited him the next morning.

He stole a secret glance at the girl. She paid him no attention. Water dripped from her hair. There was something about her, a strange familiarity Cal couldn't place.

"Do I know you?"

The girl said nothing.

Real talkative.

"You want a beer?"

It was cold in the car now, and he cranked up the heating. It had little effect. He checked the windows to make sure they were all closed.

"The name's Cal, by the way. What's yours?"

"Jenifer," she said softly, almost a whisper.

"Jenifer. I like it. It's a pretty name." He smiled at her. "A pretty name for a pretty girl," he mused out loud.

Her lips curled into something approaching a smile.

Good. He was getting through to her.

"So what were you doing out here in the—"

"I'm cold," she said. "I'm so cold."

"Say, you're not a ghost, are you?" he laughed. "My mom used to tell me..."

He trailed off. This was not the time to be talking about his damn mom. He cleared his throat and tried again.

"Heating's up to the max. Can't understand it. Damn thing must be broken." He looked at her, and she shivered.

"I need to get out of these wet clothes," she said.

And I'd like to help you with that, he thought. His erection strained against his pants. God, he wanted to free it, the poor bastard.

"Listen, Jen — can I call you Jen? — I'm on my way to meet some old college buddies. Got a trunk full of clothes in the back. Take anything you like. We can pull over somewhere and you can—"

But she was already undressing. Cal struggled to keep his eyes on the winding road. He switched on his full beams, the light barely able to penetrate the thick darkness that had settled across the land, the enormous trees that shot by blocking the dying rays of sunlight.

She slipped off her jacket and tossed it into the back. It landed with a wet splat on the expensive leather seat beside his equally expensive Gucci suitcase. Cal only owned expensive things. Nothing good in life came cheap, or free... until now.

The girl wore a white tee. Like her skirt, it was soaked.

Cal, my man, you've hit the fucking jackpot.

He tried to stay cool. He couldn't blow it.

Yeah, something's getting blown though, huh?

He swallowed hard, facing the road, but his eyes kept darting over to the girl's body. She reached for the hem of her shirt, peeling the wet garment from her skin. As she lifted it over her head, Cal took the opportunity to throw his hand down his pants and maneuver his dick into an upright position. It felt good, his cock throbbing as he looked at the girl's breasts. Her white bra was transparent, her dark nipples visible through the lacy fabric. She tossed the shirt into the back alongside her jacket and looked up at Cal. He quickly turned away, fixing his eyes on the road, unable to prevent a sly smirk from spreading across his face.

"So, uh, yeah, like I said, I'm traveling across the country to meet my buddies. Haven't seen 'em in, oh, must be twenty years or something. We grew—"

"You can watch me," she interrupted. "It's only fair."

"I, uh—"

"If it wasn't for you, I'd still be out there."

She had a point.

Her wet skin glistened in the dashboard light as she removed her bra and sat half-naked in the passenger seat. She stared at him with an unreadable expression.

Cal licked his lips. He wanted to say something, but his throat was dry. He reached one shaking hand into his shirt pocket and pulled out a cigarette as the girl unbuttoned her skirt and slipped out of it.

"Listen," he managed to say. "There's a motel about thirty miles from here. If you like, we can—"

"Tell me about your friends."

"What?"

"Your friends. Tell me about them."

There was something about her voice. He was sure they'd met before, but where? He wouldn't forget a girl like this, especially one who was clearly a total nympho.

"Are you sure we've not met?" Had he asked that already? Had she answered? He couldn't recall. Nothing seemed to matter to him right now other than the young girl sitting opposite him in her transparent white panties and nothing else.

"Need a light?" she said.

He realized the unlit cigarette was still in his mouth.

"Sure."

"Well, I don't have one," she said, and giggled. Then she arched her back and lowered her underwear.

"Jesus Christ," said Cal. "You're really something, you know that?"

She smiled thinly. "Some people would die for me."

She kicked her panties off and sat naked like it was a normal, everyday occurrence. Cal's eyes were drawn to the patch of dark hair between her legs. "You can touch me," said the girl.

"Look, I—"

She cut him off. "I want you to touch me, Calvin."

Had he told her his full name? Fuck, he couldn't think straight. Her hand was between her legs now, rubbing softly. She let out a small gasp of pleasure.

"Touch me, Calvin. Touch me like you did before."

"If you say so," he said. *You crazy bitch,* he almost added.

He took one hand from the wheel and placed it on her thigh. It was soft and damp. The car slowed, and she looked at him with a serious expression.

"Drive faster."

Outside, it was full dark. The rain pounded unceasingly against the Mercedes. Cal leaned back in his seat as the girl twisted around to face him, her hands effortlessly working his belt loose. He lifted his ass slightly as she tugged his pants and underwear down.

"I think we should pull over," he said. "I can't see a thing out there."

She gripped his cock, running her hand up and down the shaft. "You want me to stop?"

His heart raced madly.

"No," he said in a small voice.

"I didn't think so. You never know when to stop."

He wanted to ask what she meant by that, but before the question left his lips, she was already clambering on top of him, her knees on either side of his hips. He looked at her breasts, wanting nothing more than to bury his face between them.

Thunder rumbled in the distance, and he looked up in time to see a signpost looming before him. Cal jerked the wheel, almost spinning the vehicle, the wheels sliding on the rain-slicked surface before he regained control.

"I really think we should pull over," he said.

Christ, what had happened to him? He had become such a pussy. If Garrett could see him now...

The naked girl put her lips to Cal's ear, her breath warm against his skin.

"Just relax," she said as she slid his cock inside her. "And I'll do the rest."

Cal did. He moved onto autopilot, his hands on the wheel, eyes watching the road, but his mind was elsewhere, lost in ecstasy as the girl — Christ, he couldn't even remember her name — ground her hips against him.

Concentrate, concentrate...

"You're so good," he said. "Oh God, you're so good."

She leaned back, her spine across the steering wheel, and stared at Cal.

"You don't remember me, do you?" she whispered.

"I, uh—"

"It's okay," she said, still working her hips, his cock sliding in and out of her as she massaged her clitoris. "I'm just surprised. It was an important day for me. I thought maybe you'd remember it too."

He looked past her at the road, eyes half closed. He was going to come any moment now. The danger had prolonged him, but as she lay back, breasts bouncing as the car shuddered over the uneven road, he knew it was time. He prided himself on his self-control, but this girl was something special. The way she moved was—

"Look at me," she said, and he did.

His stomach lurched violently as he looked at her face,

at her swollen and discolored eye, at the trickle of blood from her lip, at the dark bruises all around her neck, and then he smelled her perfume and it all came back to him, but it was too late, too late by far, as he...

...clamped his fingers around her neck, the girl screaming, crying, begging him to stop, but he couldn't, he couldn't stop, everyone was watching and if he stopped now they'd think he was a pussy, and they'd laugh and...

...the tree rose up behind her, getting closer, closer, and then the Mercedes hit it going seventy, the hood crumpling, the glass shattering, showering the girl's naked body in millions of broken shards, except now she wasn't there, there was nothing, just his head flying towards the wheel, a devastating impact, and then darkness.

Only darkness.

When Cal awoke, he was in more pain than he had ever experienced. The front of the vehicle was curled around a tree, smoke belching from beneath the hood. He couldn't move. His dick lay limp between his legs, stained red with blood that gushed from his broken nose.

"Help me," he said, but there was no one to hear him.

No one who cared, anyway.

Footsteps crunched nearby. He tried to tilt his head, but his body refused. From the neck down, he felt nothing but an empty numbness. The girl stood by the window, peering in. She was still naked, but now she was as pale as a corpse, her lips drained of color, her eyes dead and emotionless. He remembered now, far too late, the time they had met, those fleeting hours they had spent together.

"Please," he said. "I'm sorry."

She opened the door and gazed in at him.

"You're sorry," she said, her voice a flat monotone.

He wanted to nod, but couldn't.

She bent and scooped up a handful of broken glass, her fist clenching hard. Blood seeped from between her fingers, running down her arm in a grisly trail.

"You think that's enough," she said. It wasn't a question.

She squeezed Cal's face with her free hand, opening his mouth. With her other hand, she shoved the glass in. Cal felt the razor-sharp pieces slice his tongue, the roof of his mouth, his gums. He tried to scream and it only made things worse, spreading the shards around, his mouth filling with blood. He swallowed, the glass traveling down his esophagus, cutting him, opening him up.

"You think sorry is enough," repeated the girl. She reached over to the broken windshield and snapped a large chunk of glass from the frame.

"It'll never be enough," she said, and then she brought the glass down into Cal's face. It pierced his cheek, stabbing into his already mangled tongue. He choked, expelling bloody glass fragments from the hole in his cheek like tiny rubies. She wrenched the shard out, then attacked him again, stabbing, stabbing, tearing open his face. The tip plunged into Cal's eyeball, rupturing the soft orb. He felt the glass scrape against his skull, yet somehow he lived.

Jenifer.

It had been a long time. Twenty years, he guessed. He hadn't thought about her in at least fifteen, not since the nightmares had stopped. Hell, a man can't live with guilt *all* his life. Sometimes, you have to move on. It was a mistake, a joke that had gone too far.

Jenifer.

That fateful night at the beach house, when...

...they pinned her down, an arm each, laughing, as he...

...wanted to scream but couldn't as the girl reached down to his soft and unwilling penis. With his one remaining eye, Cal watched as she lifted it and held the tip of the blood-drenched glass shard to the base of his cock and started to slice.

"It'll never be enough," she said, as the rain continued to fall and the gurgles of the dying man faded to sweet, empty nothingness.

2

LEE STOOD BY THE TOYOTA, LEANING AGAINST THE DOOR AND wishing he was anywhere but here.

From inside the car, Anya rapped her knuckles against the window. He turned to his girlfriend as she laboriously wound the window down and leaned her head out.

"You think my plants will be okay?" she asked.

"Your what?"

She smiled. "My house plants."

"I think they'll manage to survive for a weekend, yeah."

Anya nodded, satisfied. Lee could never understand how someone could care so much about some plants.

"Oh, and did you pack your toothbrush?"

Damn.

"Uh, sure," he lied. He'd forgotten it. He always did when they went on vacation. But Anya already knew that, didn't she? He looked up at the apartment block towered over them. "Beep the horn again. Don't know what's taking him so long."

"Be patient," said Anya, and she fixed Lee with a smile

that almost soothed his nerves. "Anyone would think you didn't want to be here."

"Is it that obvious?"

She punched him playfully through the open window. "Come on, this'll be fun. You get to see your old friends again, reminisce about the good times."

"The good times," he mumbled. "Yeah, sure."

"Well, if you didn't want to go—"

"I didn't. It was *you* who wanted to go, remember?"

Anya smiled at him. "I just thought it'd be good for you. For both of us. We've been cooped up in the apartment for a year now. It'll be nice to spend some time outdoors, go for refreshing mountain walks, breathe that country air..."

It was easy for *her* to say. She'd only met Peter once, and he was on his best behavior that day. Still, it wasn't Peter he was concerned about. It was Cal and Garrett and Lucy. College friends? Sure, they had all attended the same college, and bunked together, but that didn't make them friends...

If only he hadn't told Anya about the invitation. He could have just ignored the text like he had ten years ago. Now it was the twentieth anniversary of their graduation, and like a fool he was off to spend it in Garrett's mountain cabin with Anya and four people he hadn't spoken to in two decades.

To make matters worse, Peter didn't have a car, so he would have to ride with them for the latter half of the trip. For the first time, Lee wondered what Peter had been up to in his post-college life. Had the eternal slacker got a job, settled down, found his calling?

Peter's front door opened, and he exited onto the street, a backpack slung over his shoulder and a joint clamped between his teeth, his long hair tied back in a ponytail. He wore sweatpants and a — oh christ, it *couldn't* be — a Limp Bizkit hoodie.

Limp fucking *Bizkit*.

It was as if time itself had frozen in shock.

"Toilet!" shouted Peter, throwing his arms wide and coming in for a hug.

"Don't call me that," said Lee, but Peter wasn't listening. He grabbed Lee in a bearhug and spun him around.

"Okay, put me down!" The old anger was bubbling to the surface again.

No, it's too soon. Take it easy.

Peter let go and Lee stumbled back. His foot caught the edge of the sidewalk and he fell on his ass. He felt his face reddening, then got to his feet, dusting off the back of his jeans, unwilling to look at Anya. Was she laughing at him too? Probably. Fuck, he felt like he was back in college already, with all the humiliation and hatred that entailed.

"Come on, get in the car," shouted Peter, seemingly not caring that it was six in the morning and the whole block was probably asleep. He walked to the passenger door and started to open it.

"Hey, you're in the back," said Lee.

Peter looked oddly hurt. "Okay. Mind if I smoke?"

"Yeah, whatever," sighed Lee, watching as Peter tried to fit into the back of the Toyota. He was a giant of a man, had been for as long as Lee had known him. Six-five in his socks, with the physique of a kid who spent too many hours eating snacks and playing video games. He looked remarkably similar despite the passing of twenty years, his round face showing few signs of ageing. The only give-away was the gray hair that flecked his awful ponytail.

Lee took a last look at the deserted street and considered

making a run for it, but he couldn't leave Anya alone with Peter.

You should never leave a woman alone with any of those guys...

His whole body tensed.

Don't think about it.

He suddenly realized that Peter was probably right now explaining to Anya why his nickname was Toilet, and hurried into the car.

Too late.

"Hey, remember that time you shit your pants in Professor Childs' class?"

Lee felt his toes curl. It was going to be a long drive.

He looked at Anya, who turned away, stifling a giggle. Lee shook his head and gunned the engine. "You got everything?"

A beer popped behind him.

"Everything I need," said Peter. "Want one?"

"Not right now," said Lee. He pulled out onto the road and hit the button on the sat nav that would direct him towards Garrett's cabin.

It was eight hours away.

"So I take it you never learned to drive?" said Lee.

"What do I need to drive for?" said Peter. "Driving's for fags." Then, he added with a smirk, *"No offense."*

Eight hours of this.

Anya turned in her seat to look at Peter. "I'm Anya, by the way." She glared at Lee. "Thanks for introducing me."

But Peter was too busy chugging his beer to respond. When he finished, he wound down his window and threw the empty bottle onto the sidewalk.

"Dude," snapped Lee, trying not to show his frustration. "Are you for real?"

Peter sparked up his joint and reclined across the entire back seat, resting against his backpack.

"So what you been up to?" asked Lee.

"Hey," said Peter, ignoring the question. "This dump have a CD player?"

Lee gripped the steering wheel. "You mean my car?"

"Yeah, that's what I said. This heap of shit. It's old enough to have a CD player, am I right? Hell, it's older than Mrs. Franklin. Hey, remember her? That bitch drove me fucking crazy."

"Yeah, the Dean's secretary. She died a few years back. It's crazy to think how many—"

"So, you got a CD player or not?"

"Yeah," said Lee. Was that as close as they would come to a serious adult conversation all weekend?

Probably.

Peter waved a shiny compact disc between the front seats. "Cool, put this on. I made it especially for the ride."

Lee snatched the disc from him. He ejected the CD that was currently in — a Lizzo album, one of Anya's — and shoved Peter's mix into the slot.

Christ, they were getting old.

The music started, an indecipherable toneless sound fading in. What fresh hell awaited him?

"The mix tape's a lost art," said Anya.

"The courting ritual of the nerd," smiled Lee.

"Shut up and turn that jam *up,* bitch!" said Peter, clapping his hands together, forgetting he was holding his joint and sending sparks flying through the interior of the vehicle.

"Watch the upholstery, man," said Lee, but Peter couldn't hear him, because Kid Rock's interminable anthem *Bawitdaba* was rattling the chassis of the car.

"Yeah," said Peter, banging his head in time to the music. "Fucking classic!"

"Oh Jesus."

"Remember that time we saw him live," said Peter, "and you finger banged that slut in the moshpit?"

"Come on, man!" shouted Lee. He shot an apologetic glance at Anya.

She shrugged. "Hey, none of my business what you got up to when you were in college." She was acting cool, but he knew she wouldn't like Peter's language.

Well, if she thought that was bad, just wait til she met Cal and Garrett.

A cold dread needled at his belly.

Maybe they've changed. It's been twenty years.

But even the optimistic voice that lived in his head sounded dubious.

They left the suburbs, and three hours later — when the nu-metal compilation from hell had finished and resumed playing again on an endless purgatorial loop — they were deep in Appalachian country.

Five hours to go, thought Lee.

And after that, all that remained was two-and-a-half days of reliving the bad old times with his girlfriend and three sexist, racist, homophobic jocks and a mean-spirited ex-cheerleader.

Who *wouldn't* look forward to that?

3

PAPA ROACH'S *LAST RESORT* WAS BLARING FROM THE SPEAKERS for the fifth time when Lee's phone vibrated. He dug the phone from his pocket and put it on speaker, using it as an excuse to turn the volume down on the insufferable racket. He hadn't liked this music back then, and he sure as hell didn't like it now.

Garrett's voice crackled through the tinny speaker.

"Yo Toilet, is that you?"

The imbecile in the back seat cheered.

"Yeah, it's me, Garrett," said Lee. "What's up?"

He's canceling, he's canceling.

If only.

"What kinda car you fucking assholes driving?"

Lee turned to Anya and said, "Charming as ever."

"What was that?"

"Nothing." Lee sighed. Even hearing Garrett's voice made his stomach flip. "We're in a Toyota."

"Then forget about it. The road's flooded. Not stopped raining for the last two weeks."

"So... it's off?" said Lee, failing to mask his glee.

"No way, Toilet. I'll meet you at a gas station and we can all take my van. I'll text you the info."

His van... surely not *the* van. It had to be a different one. He couldn't still be driving the same van, with the skateboarding naked girl spray-painted on the side. The idea sent a shiver down Lee's spine. It doubtlessly still stunk of pot and ugly sex.

"Are you sure, man?" he said. "We could always—"

"I'm sure. Plenty space. And if not, Lucy can sit on my lap."

He laughed at that, and so did Peter. Anya smiled at Lee, but it was tinged with regret, as if only now she realized what she was in for. Dammit, why hadn't they stayed home?

"Smell you later!" shouted Garrett, and then the line mercifully cut off.

Garrett stuffed his phone in his pocket. It'd be good to see the old gang again. He would never say it out loud, but he missed them. Well, he missed the old college days. Life had never been the same. He looked at Lucy dozing quietly in the seat next to him, and wondered if she felt the same.

He carefully opened his door so as not to wake her, then slammed it shut as hard as he could.

"Uh?" she said, her eyes snapping open. "What happened?"

"Sorry, babe. Did I wake you?"

She looked blankly at him. "I must have fallen asleep."

"Guess so. You gonna put some makeup on?"

She scowled at him. "I'm wearing makeup already."

"Yeah, but a little more? The guys haven't seen you for a long time."

"I'm not trying to impress them," she said. "Anyway, it's raining."

"You could at least put in a bit of effort. And unbutton your blouse."

"Why?"

He didn't know what to say to that. That it was important to him for his old friends to think he still had it together? For them to think that his whole life hadn't been on a downward spiral for the last twenty years?

Back then, he had the world at his feet. The most popular boy in school, with a football scholarship and a head-cheerleader girlfriend. So how had he ended up unemployed, with Lucy taking on shifts at the diner to supplement her income from coaching high school cheer squads? At least it kept her in shape. Her figure was still good and firm, although when he picked her up from school, he couldn't help comparing her to the kids she was coaching. Their breasts were firmer, and their butts hadn't yet started to sag. But they had no interest in him, despite his efforts. What seventeen-year-old wants to get with a middle-aged man with no money and a rapidly expanding beer belly?

Still, he could watch, and think about them once a week on a Friday, when Lucy would lie there with one eye on the TV as he lovelessly fucked her.

"I'm going for a smoke," she said without looking at him.

"You gonna make yourself look pretty for me?"

She glared at him. "Is it for you or your friends?"

Embarrassed, he looked away. "For me, of course."

"I know what you're doing," she said. "You want them to think that you're still the big man on campus."

"Bullshit," he said, her words stinging.

"That's why you rented the van, right? To look like we've

got money, and that you don't just slob around on the couch all day eating your weight in pizza and crying."

"I don't fucking cry," he said.

"Sure."

Lucy stepped outside, sheltering beneath her umbrella and lighting up a cigarette. He watched her through the rain-streaked window, her dirty blonde hair tied back in a ponytail when it should be newly bleached and cascading over her shoulders. Her loose-fitting blouse hid her curves, but at least her yoga pants made her butt look ten years younger.

She was right about him, of course. Lucy may have been a bimbo in high school and college, but she was damn perceptive when it came to his state of mind. He figured she knew he cheated on her. But if it kept him from harassing her every night, she was probably thankful for it.

Man, if only she wasn't here. He and the boys could get some hookers and blow and have themselves a good ol' fashioned orgy. But not now, not with Lucy tagging along, so the least she could do was make herself presentable. She was still in her thirties, for god's sake.

He wondered how Peter, Cal, and Lee were doing. Their Facebook profiles gave little away. Lee hadn't updated his in years, Cal's was mostly MAGA shit, and Peter—

The door opened and Lucy climbed in, stinking of nicotine. Garrett wrinkled his nose and started the van, heading off down the highway in the rain. They took a turnoff and drove for several miles in silence, neither of them sure how to work the radio in the rented van, instead listening to the drumming of the raindrops that never seemed to let up, the clouds looming endlessly overhead in a thick gray blanket.

"What's that?" said Lucy.

"Huh?" Garrett hadn't realized how much of a funk he

was in until she spoke. He could see nothing but the blacktop stretching lazily into the horizon, and then, before he knew it, he saw her.

The girl in white, her arm outstretched, thumbing a ride.

His heart leaped into his throat, his body constricting, jerking the wheel. The van veered towards the girl, the headlights pinning her, but she never moved.

"Garrett!" screamed Lucy.

At the last moment he spun the wheel and the van screeched past her. Garrett gazed into the rearview, watching until the girl was little more than a dwindling memory.

"Was that—"

"No," said Lucy sharply.

"But—"

"I said *no.*"

Garrett nodded, unclenching his jaw. The hairs on his arms stood up, and he took one hand from the wheel and rubbed at his forearm.

Deja vu's a bitch, he thought.

He was being foolish. Of course it wasn't her. It couldn't be. That was twenty years ago, and anyway, she was—

He cast the thought aside.

No point dwelling on ancient history.

"Just a coincidence," said Lucy as she took out another cigarette, placed it in her mouth, and lit it. Garrett normally didn't allow her to smoke in the car, but this time he didn't stop her.

"You got one for me?" he said.

She looked at him, her face phantom-white, and held out the carton with a trembling hand.

"A coincidence," he said, taking a cigarette, his first since kicking the habit five years ago. "That's all."

"I know," said Lucy, but she didn't sound like she believed it.

～

Lee followed Garrett's texted directions, the Toyota pulling in to the gas station as more black storm clouds rumbled ominously across the sky.

Garrett waved at them from his van, a thankfully respectable-looking vehicle with no spray-painted naked ladies. It was the first bit of good luck Lee had experienced all day.

The gas station itself was a rundown affair. A faded sign promised BEST GAS PRICES FOR MILES, as well as TRY OUR FAMOUS CHEEZBURGERS, next to a crude painting of what Lee supposed was a sentient cheeseburger with legs and arms, but no face.

Delicious.

Before the car had even come to a stop, Peter was opening the door and racing across the tarmac towards Garrett and Lucy.

"He left the fucking door open," grumbled Lee as the rain entered the car and drenched the interior.

"You not having a good time?" said Anya.

Lee glared at her. "Are you serious?"

A fist thumped off the windshield and Lee jumped. He looked into the grinning, vapid face of Garrett, dressed in a light blue sweater and tan slacks. He was soaken wet, but Lee remembered how Garrett refused to wear jackets.

Jackets are for bitches, he used to say, whatever the fuck that meant.

God, he hated him.

Garrett pounded his fists off the hood.

"Toilet, Toilet," he chanted. Soon, the others joined him, Peter and Lucy, forming a semi-circle of idiocy around the car, chanting, chanting, not shutting up.

"Ready?" said Lee.

Anya nodded. "Hey, I'm here. You need a break from these guys, you got me. Remember that."

"Sure," he said. Did she not realize it was her fault he was even here? He opened the door and stepped out into the rain, mindful to leave his jacket in the car.

You afraid he's gonna call you a bitch in front of Anya? Afraid he's gonna steal your girl again?

Garrett threw himself at Lee and wrapped his arms around him. Unlike Peter, he was beginning to look his age, though his blonde hair still hung in those natural waves that had driven the girls crazy back in college, something Lee knew all too well. He had bunked in the same room as Garrett, and spent many a night with his head under the pillow as the jock fucked his way through the entire college female population.

"How's it hangin', Toilet?" bellowed Garrett. "Still small and a little to the left?"

"I'm fine, man," he said. He hated the way he immediately slipped back into saying 'man' when confronted with Garrett. Anya left the car and wandered round to join them. Lee smiled. "Hey guys, I'd like you to meet—"

But Garrett had already lunged forwards and grabbed the waistband of Lee's jeans, yanking them down to his ankles.

"Yup, still hanging!" he roared.

"Fuck," said Lee, dropping into a crouch and pulling his

pants back up. "Would you grow up, we're in our fucking forties!"

Garrett just laughed at him. *Everyone* was laughing at him. Even Anya. She put her hand in front of her face, but he could see her. Garrett was going to turn her against him, and then they would end up in bed together. Perhaps Garrett would convince Lucy to join in too?

Speaking of Lucy, there she was, pointing at Lee, doubled over with hilarity.

"You've not changed, Toilet," she said, wrapping her arm around Garrett's waist. "Hey, remember that time you shit your pants in—"

"Yeah," snapped Lee. "We all remember."

"Come on, pull your pants up and grab your stuff," said Garrett. He looked at the sky and frowned. "We should leave before it gets dark. Anyone heard from Cal?"

"He left last night," said Peter. "Got a message from him saying he'd just taken the biggest shit of his life in a rest stop bathroom. Sent me a photo and everything."

"Sounds like the sort of thing Toilet would do," said Lucy.

"I would *never* do that," said an incredulous Lee.

"It's nice to finally meet you guys," said Anya, stepping fully into the group.

"I've not heard from him since yesterday either," said Garrett, refusing to acknowledge Anya's presence.

"So his phone's dead," said Lucy. "He'll meet us there."

"In his fucking Merc? He'll never make it up that road."

"What about my car?" said Lee. "I can't leave it here."

"Sure you can," said Garrett. "Already arranged with the owner of the station. For fifty bucks you can leave it round back and he'll look after it." He jerked a thumb in the direction of a reedy older man in coveralls, his face stained black with grease. He leaned against a gas pump, a lit cigarette clamped between his dry lips.

Lee turned to Garrett. "Yeah, that's not happening."

"What else you gonna do?" said Lucy. Her tone was challenging, the way it always had been. She was a real bitch back then, and Jesus H. Christ, it looked like she still was. Had no one grown up but himself? Were they all stuck in their roles? The jock and his cheerleader girlfriend, Peter and Cal the faceless hangers-on who Garrett kept around to laugh at his dumb jokes and beat up the weaker kids so he didn't have to get his hands dirty.

It was pathetic.

Just get through this weekend, and you'll never have to see them again. Ever.

Oh, how he hoped that was true.

They piled into Garrett's van, dumping their packs and suitcases in the back with Lee and Anya. Garrett, Lucy, and Peter snuggled into the front seats, and then the beers were out and open and they were on their way up the mountain to Garrett's cabin. It was just like old times.

Dammit to hell, it was *just* like old times.

"Think about the hot tub," smiled Anya.

It was sound advice.

Garrett's cabin had a hot tub and steam room, a full entertainment system, and mountain views overlooking a lake. There were kayaks, mountain bikes, nature trails... It would be idyllic if they didn't have to share it with people he hated. Particularly the hot tub. Lee hoped to find a private moment in there with Anya. She had been cool with him in bed lately. Distant, frigid.

He couldn't blame her. Ever since he had agreed to come on the trip, his mood had darkened. He felt himself returning to his old ways. Back then, in his college days, he had what some referred to as an 'anger management problem'. At the time he had thought everyone was full of shit, but with the benefit of hindsight, he supposed they had a point. He had been liable to fly into rages, blind furies where everything else seemed to fade into insignificance. Over the last twenty years, he thought he had beaten it, calmed down... but recently, the red mist had begun descending again at the slightest infraction, the merest hint of an insult or slight.

He looked at Anya and felt for her. No one was paying her a blind bit of attention. Any time she asked a question, she was met with stony silence. It was fucking hostile. His fists clenched.

Cool it. Cool it.

At least Peter's CD was still in the Toyota. If he had to listen to Linkin Park one more fucking time, he would snap and go on a murder spree.

Calm down.

He was trying to. But everything was annoying him. The rain on the window, the sound of rattling beers inside one of Garrett's bags, the way his wet collar rubbed his neck...

All he wanted was to get into bed. He didn't even care if Anya was with him or not.

He just wanted to sleep and get this over with.

4

THE GANG WAS DRUNK ALREADY, AND THEY HADN'T EVEN arrived.

Garrett and Peter downed their drinks, spilling most of their Coronas — Garrett thought it was hilarious to drink Corona after the previous year — down their clothes. He finished first, and with one hand on the wheel, crushed the can against his forehead and yelled. Lucy clapped and hugged him, the van veering wildly off the road for several heart stopping seconds.

"Careful, man," said Lee. "I wanna get there in one piece."

Anya snuggled closer to him.

"You want a drink?" she said.

"Really?"

She shrugged. "If you can't beat 'em, join 'em, right?"

He almost laughed. "Sure," he said. "Why the fuck not?"

"We're gonna get through this," she whispered. "You and me together, and fuck the rest of them."

"You see why I didn't want to come now?"

She leaned closer and kissed him on the cheek. "It's gonna be okay. Just keep repeating, *hot tub, hot tub, hot tub.*"

Lee did laugh this time, and Peter glanced over his shoulder at him. "You're weird, man," he said, then turned back. Lee didn't understand what he meant, but neither did he care. Let the group ostracize them. It was no loss. Then he and Anya could spend time alone, in bed or in the hot tub. God knows, they needed it to rekindle the dwindling fire of their sexual relationship. The idea of Anya in a jacuzzi, naked and willing... he felt his groin stir.

"What's wrong?" said Anya, and then she realized. "Really?" she said, smiling.

"It's the vibrations," he said, and now she was laughing. It was a delightful sound, one he hadn't heard enough recently. He moved in to kiss her, and—

The brakes screeched. Lee's teeth smacked off Anya's.

"Jesus fuck!" he heard Garrett scream, the van tipping forwards as if suddenly they were going downhill. Peter scrambled into the back as Lee looked through the windshield and saw a yawning chasm opening up before them, a river thundering through a valley hundreds of feet below.

"The fucking bridge," yelled Garrett, following Peter over the seat and into the back. "Get out, we're gonna fall!"

The van kept tipping, halting only when Garrett and Peter reached the back doors. The weight seemed to even out, the vehicle rocking gently back and forth. Only Lucy was still in the front. She couldn't seem to stop screaming.

"What's going on?" said Lee, his voice shrill and panicky.

"The bridge is gone," said Garrett.

"We're going to die," wailed Lucy. "We're going to fucking die!"

"Babe, calm down," said Garrett. "I'm coming for you." He crawled towards her, and Lee grabbed him by the hem of his shirt as the van rocked again, the back wheels lifting off the ground. Lucy screamed, her voice piercing.

"Don't move," said Lee. "We need to keep the weight at the back." Garrett turned to face him, his eyes wide with fear.

"That's my girl," he said.

"I know, but—"

Something cracked beneath them, the van sliding forwards.

"I'm getting out of here," said Peter, reaching for the back door handle. Lee shuffled to the side, blocking him.

"You can't! Not until we get Lucy up here with us."

Peter was the heaviest person present. Without him to even things out, they would go over the edge.

Lucy had stopped screaming. Now she sniveled and sobbed, retreating into a ball in the middle seat. Lee glanced out the back window for signs of an approaching vehicle, anything to save them. What he saw instead was a figure.

A girl, clad in rain-soaked white, watching them.

Lee flung open the door.

"Hey!" he shouted. "Help!"

"What're you doing?" said Garrett. "We gotta get Lucy out!"

The van groaned.

Lee watched as the rain pummeled the girl, her dark hair sticking to her face. Then she turned and walked slowly away.

"Hey, come back!" shouted Lee.

"There's no one there!" said Garrett. He turned to Lucy. "Babe, you're gonna have to come to us. We can't move."

The apocalyptic downpour drowned out her whimpered response.

The van slid forwards again. Any further and it'd be

vertical. After that, the only way was down. A *long* way down.

"Lucy," said Lee. "Listen to me. Garrett's right, you have to come to us, and you have to do it *now*."

"Please," said Anya. "We've got you."

"Come on, babe," said Garrett. "Be strong."

Her face appeared between the seats, makeup running in black rivers down her cheeks.

"I can't," she said.

Lee glanced to the road again. The girl in white was gone.

Concentrate, dammit.

"Come on, you can do it," he said to Lucy. She shook her head.

"We're moving, man," said Peter. "We gotta get out."

"Not without Lucy," snapped Garrett.

But Peter was right. The van creaked, slipping, and then Garrett did the unthinkable. He rushed towards the front seats.

"Stop!" said Lee. Anya screamed. The van tipped forwards. Lee watched as Garrett seemed to move in slow motion, grabbing his girlfriend's outstretched arm and hauling her over the front seats.

Time was up.

"Get out," said Lee to Anya. She leaped from the van, Peter following.

"Lee, come on," cried Anya, tears in her eyes.

Garrett dragged Lucy up the steadily increasing incline. Lee felt himself rising higher and higher as the vehicle tipped dangerously forwards. Now the only things stopping them from tumbling into the ravine were himself and some suitcases. He reached his hand out and Garrett took it, his grip sweaty and loose, and then the van was falling. Lee hurled himself back, taking Garrett with him. He fell from the van, landing heavily in the thick wet mud, clinging on desperately to Garrett's slippery hand. From his low vantage point, Lee couldn't see if Garrett was still holding on to Lucy. It sure felt like it. The weight was immense, and Lee knew he couldn't hold on for long. He dug his heels in to the mud, but there was no grip. He slid towards the chasm as the rain battered his face and body, knowing he was going to die, and then there were hands on him, pulling him backwards to safety.

"I got you," said Peter.

Lee concentrated all his remaining strength into holding on to Garrett. He looked down and saw the man's mud-caked face between his legs. Did he still have Lucy?

Yes, he could hear her screaming in terror. Moments later, the sound of the van hitting the bottom of the chasm reverberated across the land, a dreadful crunch like a miniature atomic bomb.

Anya hovered over Lee. He felt like his arm had popped out of its socket. She leaned over him, kissing him, not caring that his face was covered in wet filth.

Lucy crawled as far from the edge as she could manage, while Garrett looked out over towards the chasm.

"Shit, man," he said. He turned to Lee, and sighed. "There go the beers."

Lee didn't know if it was due to the delirium of having survived a close encounter with death or not, but he couldn't help himself.

He burst out laughing.

5

THE FIVE OF THEM TRUDGED WEARILY DOWN THE ROAD.

There was nothing else to do. The bridge was gone, the ravine impassable, and the van with all their belongings lay in pieces at the foot of it. Only Lee had his phone on him when they went over the edge, but so far he was struggling to find a signal.

No wonder. They were on a mountain, surrounded by thick Blue Ridge forest.

"Maybe when we get closer to civilization," he said, pocketing the phone. He was drenched. The rain had at least washed most of the mud away, but Lee had never been a glass-half-full kinda guy. Anya held onto his hand, shivering in jeans and a sweater. Despite the downpour, he could tell she was crying.

"Where are we going?" said Peter. "There ain't nothing around for miles."

"You got a better idea?" said Garrett.

Apparently Peter didn't.

"The girl I saw had to have come from somewhere," said Lee. "She wasn't dressed for this weather."

"Yeah, the girl that no one else saw," said Peter.

"I saw her," said Anya quietly.

"You did?" said Lee.

She nodded and gripped his hand tighter.

Garrett turned to Lee and gave him an askew glance. "We didn't pass anything on the way up here. The nearest building is the gas station, and that's at least a five-hour hike down the mountain."

"Then we'll have to find somewhere to shelter," said Lee.

"Like where?"

"I don't know. We can build one."

"I know how to do that," said Anya.

Garrett just shook his head and clung on to Lucy. The girl stumbled, her foot sticking in the mud, and Lee noticed she was wearing heels.

Jesus, he thought. Yoga pants and heels, quite the combination.

Peter sneezed, and it echoed for miles.

"Shit, we're alone out here," said Lee.

"What if a bear attacks us?" said Lucy. It was the first words she'd spoken in a long time.

"They're drawn by the smell of food," said Garrett. "And we don't have any."

"No shortage of water though," said Lee, wiping a sodden arm across his brow. "If it stops raining, we can just wring our clothes out."

"I'm glad you can make jokes," said Peter. "Personally, I'd—"

But something had caught Lee's eye. A light between the trees. Faint, for sure, but a light nonetheless.

"You see that?" said Lee.

Anya's grip on his hand tightened. "Oh my god," she breathed.

"I can't see anything," said Garrett.

Lee pointed through the darkness. "There, a fucking light! You see it?"

"Holy shit, we're saved!" said Garrett. "Lucy, look!"

He immediately peeled off the road and the others followed him through the forest, their feet squelching through the wet soil and sludge. Sometimes the light would momentarily vanish like a cruel illusion, but then it resumed, a glowing beacon for the five weary and drenched travelers.

Soon, they emerged into a clearing. Set in the center was an incongruous-looking building that to Lee's eyes resembled some kind of long-abandoned southern mansion, two floors of filthy white stone and ostentatious pillars. Vines hung from the roof, vegetation sprouting along the ruined walls.

"What the fuck," he said, gazing up at the uninviting structure.

"It looks like it should be on a plantation," said Anya. She and Lee exchanged worried glances.

"Who do you think lives here?" said Peter.

Lucy turned to face him. "Who cares? Let's get out of this fucking rain." She looked at Garrett and said, "Good thing I put on all that makeup, huh?"

"Don't start," he said.

Lucy ignored him and strode through the ferns, brushing the waist-high plants aside. A small staircase led up to a porch, and she stopped before it.

"You guys coming or not?"

"She's right," said Anya. "Why are we standing out here?"

Still no one moved.

Lee scanned the surrounding area. There was no driveway, no way to access the property without trudging through the woods halfway up a mountain.

"I don't like this," he said quietly to Anya.

"It'll be fine," she said. "What's the worst that could happen?"

"They could kill us all with a shotgun." He was only half-joking.

"What was that, Toilet?" said Garrett.

"Nothing. Come on, let's see who's home."

They cautiously approached. A couple of rooms were lit, one on the first floor and one on the second. Shadow figures flitted by them now and again, shapeless and ethereal. The warm orange glow of the lights did little to set Lee's mind at ease.

This wasn't right.

The house shouldn't be here.

It didn't belong.

He didn't know how else to say it.

It simply *did not belong here*.

PART II

Welcome Home

6

THEY STOOD BY THE DOOR, WAITING FOR SOMEONE TO MAKE the first move.

Up close, the mansion was in a dreadful state of disrepair. The white paint was chipped and peeling, long black stains dripping from the roof like mascara tears. It smelled funny too, *old* somehow, like musty clothing discovered in a box in an attic.

From inside came the distant strains of old jazz music, because *of course* it did.

"You gonna knock?" said Lucy.

Garrett glanced nervously at her. They were shielded under the porch awning, but their clothes dripped steadily onto the boards. His sweater sleeves hung below his hands, distended and malformed.

"Yeah, I'll knock," he said definitively, then pushed his way to the front of the group. He hammered his knuckles three times off the door and stepped back, waiting.

The music stopped, a needle scratching off a record.

They waited, huddling together to stay warm.

"Someone's coming," whispered Anya.

Footsteps shuffled down a hallway. A bolt was withdrawn, and then the door opened, light spilling out across the porch.

"Good heavens," said a voice. "Visitors, at this hour!"

It was a woman. Lee figured her for mid-to-late-sixties, her face well lived in. She was dressed head to toe in black, but there was a kindness to her eyes, the way she looked upon them like they were foolish children.

"We're sorry to bother you," he said, "but we were in an accident."

"Our van went into the ravine," said Garrett. "We lost everything. You have a phone we could use?"

The woman looked them over. Lee shirked back in embarrassment. They must have been a pitiful sight. She nodded to herself, mulling something over.

"You all need to come inside right now," she said. "Why, you'll catch your death of cold out there!"

"Really, we don't—" started Anya, before Lucy spoke over her.

"We're grateful for the hospitality, ma'am."

The woman stood back to allow access to the property, and Lucy was the first through the door. Lee looked at Anya and shrugged. The woman's easy-going manner had calmed his frayed nerves, for the time being at least. Later, he could reflect on the fact that earlier that day, they had all almost *died*.

But not now. Now, he was warm, and could smell meat sizzling from a kitchen somewhere. The woman seemed to notice his interest.

"I was just making supper for my girls," she said, her face crumpling into a wrinkled smile. "I'm sure they'd be delighted if you'd join us. We don't get many visitors out here." She shook her head. "No, not many visitors at all."

"That's very kind of you," said Lee. "But do you have a phone?"

"Oh, no phone here," laughed the woman, as if he had just made the world's funniest joke. "Goodness gracious, no. What business would I have with a telephone?" Tears rolled down her cheeks. "Who would I call? The Queen of England?"

"Say," said Peter. "What's this about *your girls?*"

The woman abruptly stopped laughing. The smile fell from her face, a faraway stare coming over her.

"My girls," she said absently. "My daughters." She looked over her shoulder and took a deep breath.

"Patricia!" she screamed at the top of her lungs. *"Bethany!"*

The group exchanged bemused glances.

The woman clasped her hands in front of her. "I'd better go and get them. Young ladies can be so lazy these days, don't you think?"

The question wasn't addressed to anyone in particular, and Lee assumed it was rhetorical. The woman trotted down the sparsely furnished hall, resting against a wicker cane. She stopped a moment and turned back.

"My name is Mrs. Marcus," she said. "But you may call me... Mrs. Marcus."

Then she vanished through a door, and all was silent, save the sinister drumming of the rain against the porch.

Garrett's voice dropped to a whisper. "What the fuck did she just say?"

Lee snorted out a laugh. *"My name is Mrs. Marcus, but you can call me... Mrs. Marcus."*

Anya elbowed him sharply. "Lee," she hissed. "That's rude."

"She's fucking crazy, right?" said Garrett.

"What are her daughters gonna look like?" said Lucy.

"I hope they're hot," said Peter. They turned to look at him, and he shrugged. "What? I nearly died. I'm fucking *horny.*"

"That's great to know," said Lee.

"Just keeping you all up-to-date."

Lee shook his head, but he secretly understood. He felt it too, a weird desire to fuck. He put it down to the near-death experience, but really, it hadn't started until he set foot in the house.

Nothing more arousing than the faded grandeur of ruined plantation houses, right?

He smiled and moved closer to Anya, resting his hand on her ass. She smelled of wet clothes, and he realized he wanted her very badly indeed. He slid his hand down the back of her jeans, and her cold, clammy skin reminded him of the way she felt after sex.

The door at the end of the hallway opened. A small gust whistled down the hall. The lights flickered, and he noticed for the first time that the room was lit only by candles. Perhaps they had no electricity out here? It would make sense. No electricity, no need for a phone.

"Shit," muttered Peter under his breath, as two young women filed into the hall, each carrying a dripping red candle that illuminated them with a soft glow. They walked towards the group, cupping one hand over their flames, moving in perfect synchronization. They could almost pass for twins. Both had black hair that hung to their shoulders, and wore matching white gowns that appeared tantalizingly translucent in the glow of their candles.

"Hello," said the first girl. "I'm Patricia."

"And I'm Bethany," said the second.

Peter stepped forwards to introduce himself. "The name's Peter. A pleasure to meet you both."

"Pleased to meet you, Mr. Peter," said Patricia.

"We're pleased to meet *all* of you," said Bethany. "Mother says you'll be staying for supper."

She spoke like she was reading from a script at gunpoint.

"That's very kind," said Lee. "Is there anywhere we could dry off?"

Bethany looked at him and smiled vacantly. He found himself bizarrely attracted to the girl. She had an innocence, a naivety to her that beguiled him. He felt it in his pants. Funny, the pair of them no longer looked alike. Bethany's hair was actually dark red, her mouth smaller, her eyes brown rather than Patricia's dusky blue irises. It must have been a trick of the light.

"Mother's preparing your rooms," she said.

"Our rooms?" said Peter.

"Yes, of course," interjected Patricia. "You'll stay for supper, and be our guests overnight."

Bethany looked at her sister. "And then in the morning..."

She trailed off, the two girls dissolving into a fit of giggles.

"In the morning...?" said Garrett.

The girls stared at him.

"Come," said Patricia sharply. "We'll show you to your rooms."

The old woman moved silently down the hallway, her feet seeming to glide across the floor. She made her way through to the room at the rear of the house, the one that was usually locked.

But not today.

Not when there were more visitors.

She pushed open the door, and the man inside looked at her.

"Please," he said, teardrops rolling down his ravaged cheeks. "Let me go."

Mrs. Marcus laughed at that. She walked to the table, upon which lay her tools and implements. *Her spread,* as she called it.

"You're in luck, Mr. Huston," she said, her hand hovering over a mallet. She smiled. No, a mallet wouldn't do. It would be too easy, too painless. "More guests have arrived."

"I won't tell anyone, I swear," the man blubbered, his hands above his head, bound together and attached to a hook that dangled from a chain. He wore nothing but piss-stained underpants around his ankles.

"Oh, I believe you wouldn't," she said. "You're good at keeping secrets, aren't you?" She picked up a screwdriver, turned it over in her hand. "After all, your wife still doesn't know about the girl you raped behind the train station, does she? And I bet she's not aware of the mess you made of poor Lara that night in the park." She turned to the man, clutching the screwdriver. "You left her in pieces, didn't you?"

"I'm sorry, I didn't mean for it to happen. I was drunk, I—"

"Were you surprised to see young Lara again?"

He gazed at her, his face full of ragged holes. "What is this place?" he sobbed.

"Why, this is my home for wronged women," she said. "Didn't you know that?"

Then she raised the screwdriver and plunged it into the man's forehead. She ripped it out and blood fountained, gushing from the fresh wound, drenching her hair and clothes. The man screamed. It was funny how long they were able to scream, even after they should be dead.

His feet kicked against the restraints, but they were slowing.

She wondered how many times she could stab him before he died.

Mrs. Marcus smiled.

There was only one way to find out.

7

THEY FOLLOWED THE TWO GIRLS UP THE STAIRS.

Lee glanced around. The exterior of the building hadn't prepared him for the grand opulence on display within. The place was pristine, with thick carpets that appeared to have never been trodden on, and antique-looking walnut furniture displaying exquisite craftsmanship. Everything about the place looked either brand new or recently renovated. It reminded him of a museum. He half-expected the paintings and ornaments to be roped-off to keep curious hands from touching them.

The girls stopped outside the first door, its brass handle shining and unmarred by fingerprints.

"This will be your room," one of them said to Garrett and Lucy. "We'll be along soon with some clothes for you to change into."

"What about me?" said Garrett. "You got anything for men?"

"I think you'd look pretty in a little summer dress," said Lucy.

"I'm sure we'll find something suitable for a big, strong

man like you," said Patricia, looking at her sister as she did so.

Garrett beamed an enormous smile at her, and Lucy practically dragged him into the room.

"What time's dinner?" he said, shaking free of Lucy. "I'm starving."

"When you hear the bell, supper will be served."

Lee turned to Anya and mouthed *the bell* at her. Anya raised her eyebrows.

"This way please," said Bethany, motioning for the others to follow.

She swept past Lee, her hand accidentally brushing his crotch.

Accidentally?

It must have been.

They passed three more doors until they came to a stop. Bethany looked apologetically at Peter. "I'm afraid we don't have enough rooms for you all," she said. "So you'll have to sleep in *my* room. I hope you don't mind."

Peter's jaw visibly dropped. "And, uh... where will *you* sleep?"

"With Patricia of course, silly," said Bethany.

"Gee, I'm sorry," said Peter, and Bethany shushed him by holding a delicate finger to his lips.

"No need to apologize," she said. "My sister and I often sleep together."

Peter looked like he was on the verge of making a joke, then thought better of it.

"This is a pretty big house you've got," said Lee. "Surely there's a spare room for Peter?"

Bethany looked guilelessly at him. "No, there isn't," was all she said.

"Hey, it's okay," said Peter. "I don't mind."

"Perfect," said Bethany. "Let me show you."

She took Peter by the hand and led him inside, the door slamming shut behind them.

Patricia looked at Lee and Anya.

"And you two come with me, please."

The light from her candle flickered, casting strange shadows across her pretty face. She walked further down the hallway. The damn thing never seemed to end, just door after door, painting after painting, like the looped background in an old *Scooby Doo* cartoon.

"This is very kind of you," said Anya.

"Oh, no trouble at all," replied the girl. She turned and fixed Anya with a stare. "I think you'll really like it here."

They passed more doors. How many doors *were* there?

"I think I'll need a map to find my way back," said Lee.

Patricia stared at him. "We don't have a map," she said.

"No, it was a, uh, joke. Y'know?"

"Yes," she said. "A joke. But there's no map."

Lee nodded. "Okay. But I wasn't being seri—"

"Your room," said Patricia.

Anya stepped forwards. "Thank you. You're most gracious hosts."

The girl looked unsure for a moment, then stepped forwards and hugged Anya.

"Oh!" said Anya. She looked at Lee, then gingerly put her arms around the younger woman. Patricia released her, then glanced nervously at Lee.

"I'm sorry, I shouldn't have done that," she said, then scurried off down the hall.

Lee watched as she ran down the endless corridor, except now it was normal length. She passed two doors, and then took a right down the staircase to the entrance. He couldn't understand it.

"Hey," he said.

Anya turned to him. "What's up?"

But he couldn't articulate it. What he was trying to say made no sense.

No sense at all.

"Come on," said Anya. She sounded cheery, all things considered. "Let's check out our room."

"Yeah," he said, staring down the hallway.

Two doors, and then the staircase.

How? They must have passed dozens of the damn things. He could have sworn—

"Lee?"

He glanced into the room. Anya stood in her bra and panties, her wet clothes in a pile on the floor beside her.

"You coming?" she said with a smile.

"Do you like my room?" asked Bethany.

Peter looked at her soft features and sweet smile. "I like it a lot."

"Thank you. I decorated it myself."

Peter grinned. "I wasn't talking about the room."

Bethany giggled, hiding her mouth as she did so.

"How old are you?" he asked.

"A lady never tells, that's what Mrs. Marcus says."

"You mean your mom?"

She looked momentarily confused. "Yes. My... my *mother.*"

On a different day, the hesitation in her voice may have alerted Peter to something. But not today, not when all he could think about was what was beneath Bethany's thin white gown.

"I like you," he said, and she giggled again. She giggled a lot. Peter liked when she did. It made him think about the noises she would make when she came. "I feel bad though, making you sleep somewhere else." He gestured to the wooden four poster bed. "There's plenty of room for two."

The girl bit her lip and looked at the floor.

"The bathroom's that way," she said, pointing past him to a door.

An en-suite. Nice. He wondered if the others had the same?

"Why don't you take a shower, and I'll bring you some dry clothes?"

Peter nodded, and put his hand on her waist. He could feel her goose-pimpling flesh through the flimsy material of the nightgown.

"Sure," he said. "If I'm in the shower when you come back, just let yourself in."

He looked into her eyes, and it was the damnedest thing. She looked somehow different... familiar. His hands reached for the buttons on her gown. She didn't stop him. He undid the first one, exposing a small amount of white flesh. The second button revealed a necklace, a small gold heart on the end. He reached for the third, his clumsy hands scraping the top of her breasts, and she pulled away.

"I have to go now," she said.

He stared at her. "You look like someone I used to know."

"Nonsense," said Bethany. "I look like me."

Then she turned and ran from the room, her bare feet soundless on the carpeted floor. Her perfume lingered, and Peter breathed it in, overcome with an aching sense of nostalgia.

Fuck, she looked *exactly* like his step-sister.

8

———

PETER STEPPED INTO THE SHOWER, LETTING THE WATER WASH over his body. It was lukewarm, but better than nothing. He wondered if Bethany would come back. He thought she would. The way she had looked at him... the dumb bitch couldn't resist him.

It was weird how much she resembled his step-sister Melissa. Like, *really* fucking weird.

He rubbed the fresh bar of soap over his chest and under his armpits, the suds running down his chest to his dick. He ran his hand over it, thinking about Melissa, and started to stroke himself.

No, better wait. Bethany will be back soo—

A knock at the bathroom door.

"Hot damn," he muttered. "Horny little slut can't *wait* to take a ride on the Peter pole."

The Peter pole? Jeez, he hadn't called it that in years. To be fair, he hadn't had sex in the last, what... eight or nine years? A decade? He had lost count. Peter preferred staying in his basement playing video games and browsing the internet to going out these days. He had found a group of friends online, like-minded souls who were also involuntarily celibate, and spent much of his time—

Three more knocks. Jesus, was he gonna let her in or not?

But wait. What if it wasn't her… what if it was the old lady? Or Garrett playing a prank? The more he thought about it, the less likely it seemed that Bethany would be attracted to him. Women had always despised him, ridiculed and humiliated him. His step-sister Melissa had done that. That bitch—

Another knock, sharper this time.

The water whirled down the plughole. He pulled back the shower curtain and poked his head out. Steam filled the room, and he waved it away.

"Who's there?"

No answer. The bathroom door remained closed.

No, wait.

The handle was turning.

"That you, Beth?"

It moved all the way down, then clicked.

The door opened slightly.

Bethany entered.

"I brought your clothes," she said.

Peter relaxed. So she *was* into him.

"I'll leave them on the bed," she said.

"Just bring 'em in," he said, his heart pounding. He rubbed his dick a little to make it bigger.

Gotta look my best, he thought. *Big, but not too big. Leave some surprise for her.*

"I hope they fit," she said. Without looking at him, she padded along the tiled floor and laid the folded garments on the toilet seat. Finally, she turned to him.

"Fuck," he gasped. It was like he had gone back in time.

His step-sister stood there, looking intently at him. But not Melissa now, no... it was Melissa twenty-something years ago, when she was eighteen and he was fifteen. He remembered the way he used to spy on her in the shower, watching through a crack in the door and jerking off. She was the first girl he'd ever seen naked, his forbidden fruit. It was perverse, he knew that. It was *wrong*. One time he'd told Garrett about it when they were drunk, and even Garrett had told him he was a creep.

"That's your sister, bro," Garrett had said.

"My step-sister. We're not related."

Thankfully, Garrett had forgotten about it the next day.

"Do you need a towel?" she asked.

"Yeah, I do."

He thought about pulling the shower curtain all the way back. Was that too forward? Hell, he was naked and she was in the same room. How much more forward could he be?

She picked up a towel and came to him.

Jesus, she was the absolute spitting image of Melissa. He looked down at his fully erect penis, and then she was there, drawing the curtain back.

"I brought your towel," she said, and goddammit, her *voice* was the same too.

"Melissa," he whispered, though he knew it couldn't be.

"You can call me whatever you want," she said in Melissa's voice, as she stepped into the tub with him. He moved back, the water pouring over her gown, soaking it to her skin. She moved close, her breasts pressing against him. He kissed her, his oldest fantasy coming to life. He had *hated* Melissa. He remembered the time she and her friends had caught him looking through her underwear drawer, and she had spanked his bare ass in front of them while they sat around laughing and taking photos.

"You bitch," he said as she kissed his neck, his chest, her hands finding his penis. She stroked it gently, then got on her knees, looking up at him with big doe eyes, his small cock pointing at her face.

He gripped the handrail, his legs turning to jello as she—

"What are you doing?" shrieked a voice.

Mrs. Marcus.

Melissa spun in his arms as Mrs. Marcus stormed into the room, coming for the girl. Peter tried to cover his hard dick with his hands as the old lady wrenched her out of the tub by her arm.

"I'm sorry," cried the girl as the older woman manhandled her to her feet.

Peter watched in disbelief. He slowly pulled the curtain back along to hide his nakedness.

"Wicked girl," said Mrs. Marcus. "Beastly, wicked girl!" She dragged Melissa — no, wait, her name was Bethany, wasn't it? — over to the toilet and sat herself down, pulling the girl over her knee. "Such a way to behave in front of our guests!"

"No, please!" cried the girl.

Peter didn't know what to do. Should he say something? Tell the old lady it was his fault?

Fuck *that.*

Let Melissa take her punishment after all these years.

The old lady pulled Melissa's wet gown up past her ass.

"I'll teach you a lesson in manners," she said, and started to spank her.

"What the fuck," whispered Peter.

Melissa whimpered and cried as the hard whacks of flesh-on-flesh resounded through the room. Without realizing it, he started to rub his dick.

"Fuck you, Melissa," he said, and started to laugh. "See how *you* like it."

Mrs. Marcus deposited her on the floor and the girl crawled away, rubbing gently at the tender skin.

"I'm sorry you had to see that," said Mrs. Marcus.

"I'm not," said Peter. He was seconds away from coming. He took a last look at Melissa's crying, tear-streaked face, and then he did, his semen splattering the shower curtain.

The old woman looked at the thick fluid dribbling down the curtain, and shook her head. "Boys will be boys," she said with a wry smile, and left the room, leaving Melissa on the floor.

Peter stepped out of the shower, his dick still dripping. He looked down at Melissa. It was her, all right. She hadn't aged a day in twenty-five years.

What's going on?

Was he hallucinating? Was this house fucking with him?

Who cares?

"You're finally going to get what you deserve, you little bitch," he said. She shuffled away from him, her gown bunched up around her waist.

"Please, don't," she said. "Please..."

He loomed over her, grabbing her gown and ripping it up over her head, leaving her naked. Her hands shot down to cover her pubic area.

"All those years, flaunting your body in front of me, like you were too good for me. Making fun of me in front of your friends. Well, who's laughing now?"

He took her by the shoulders and shook her, his dick flapping in front of her face.

"Well, now I'm gonna take what's rightfully mine."

She was no longer crying. Instead, she looked up at him with cold, savage eyes.

"My sister won't be happy with you."

"I don't give a shit about your sister."

She smiled, and it chilled him to the bone.

"You should. Jenifer has quite a temper."

Jenifer.

The name meant something to him.

Jenifer.

"Get up," he said.

"She's very angry with you."

He slapped her hard across the face. She didn't react.

"Yeah, well your sister's not here, is she?" he said.

She looked at him funny.

"Yes, she is. She's right behind you."

"There's no one—"

But then he could feel it, the cold breath on his neck. A presence, behind him, the way he...

...stood behind her, clutching her arms so hard he knew it would leave marks, but what they were about to do was always going to leave a mark, there was no way around it, as she struggled, the others laughing at her, partly because they were drunk, and partly because they wanted it to happen, and the girl screamed again as Peter draped her naked body over the table, Cal holding her wrists, and then he thrust his...

...cock had lost its hardness. He didn't want to turn round, because part of him knew who would be standing there, the girl from way back when, the one they had—

"Why did you do it, Peter?" said the voice from behind, and then someone pushed him.

"Jesus," he had time to say, before the small of his back cracked against the ceramic toilet bowl, jolting his spinal column. He collapsed on the floor, turning to face his attacker, knowing full well who he would see.

She stood before him, as naked as the last time he'd seen

her, when he'd left her bleeding and weeping, watching as someone stepped forwards to take his place behind her.

"No," he said. "You're dead."

"That's not going to stop me."

Peter started to cry. "It was so long ago."

She nodded sadly. "For me, it was a lifetime ago."

She lifted the cistern lid and raised it above her head.

"Don't," he whimpered, as she brought the lid down, gravity doing most of the work. He held his arms up to shield the blow, but his bones were useless, shattering on impact. He screamed, and screamed, and screamed, hoping one of his friends would hear him.

"Shout all you want," said the girl. "There's...

...no one around to hear you, said Peter, as his thighs smacked repeatedly off her ass, and then he picked her panties off the floor and shoved them in...

...his mouth until he gagged.

"How do you like it?" she said. His arms dangled pathetically by his side, his own balled-up underwear in his mouth, choking him, the taste making him want to vomit. He did so, the bile spewing forth from the sides of his mouth, and then she and Bethany were lifting him, lying his stomach across the toilet seat, his forehead touching the chilly tiles.

"Mmmmmphh," he said, tears falling from his eyes. He felt hands on his ass, spreading his cheeks wide, and watched as Bethany lifted a large chunk of splintered ceramic and handed it to the figure behind him, the one who twenty years ago he had raped and left for dead.

"I think he's trying to say something," said Bethany. She reached two fingers into his mouth and pulled out his crumpled underpants. More vomit spilled out, spattering the floor, the smell unbearable.

"It wasn't just me," he spluttered.

"I know that," said the girl.

Jenifer.

"I've already spoken with Cal."

Peter sobbed.

Jenifer pressed something between his cheeks, gracelessly prodding the ceramic shard into his asshole. He wailed, he kicked, but still she kept pushing until his anus tore open and the large piece disappeared inside him.

"Another," said Jenifer.

Bethany grinned as she handed a second fragment of the cistern lid to Jenifer.

Peter's eyes went wide. "No, no, no! You can't do this to m—"

But they could, and they did.

Blood gushed down the valley between his ass cheeks, his torn asshole hemorrhaging great gouts of ichorous fluid. It washed across the floor, filling the gaps between the ornate blue tiles. He could feel the pieces inside him, clanking off each other, cutting and slicing him.

"All I wanted was a ride to the nearest town," she said. "That's all I wanted." She shoved another piece into him. "Why did you do it?"

But he was beyond listening now, her voice white noise, the distant crackle of an old radio. He slid off the toilet and landed on his side, feeling the strangest sensation in his stomach and bowels. He looked up at Jenifer and saw her holding one last piece of ceramic. She spread his legs and took his quickly retreating member in her hands.

"I wonder if I can fit a piece in here?" she said, and smiled.

It turned out she could.

9

"GUESS WE SHOULD GET DRESSED," SAID LEE. "IT'LL BE supper soon."

Anya ran her fingers through his chest hair. "At the toll of the bell, right?"

"That's right," he smiled, putting his arm around her, letting her rest her head on his bare chest. The sex had been good. Great, in fact. He felt spent, and wanted nothing more than to close his eyes and fall asleep.

"Think she's got a car?" he said, stretching languorously.

"Who?"

"The old lady. How else are we gonna get into town tomorrow?"

"Never really thought about it," said Anya.

He turned to her. "I thought you'd be more..."

"More what?"

He struggled to find the words. "More upset. We could have died back there."

"But we didn't." Her hand slid down to his belly, and kept going.

He didn't press the matter, not as her hand found his

cock. He hadn't seen Anya like this in weeks. It was like she had experienced a sexual reawakening. Could a near-death experience bring that about? Sex and death were so intertwined that it was only natural someone would seek out pleasures of the flesh when they came so close to losing it all.

Feeling philosophical today?

He supposed so, lying back as Anya rolled on top of him, letting the covers fall off her, beads of perspiration from their last session visible on her stomach.

"You're fucking insatiable," he said.

"It's this house. Ever since we came inside, I feel..."

"You feel what?"

"I don't know," she said. "Different. I feel different."

She perched on her knees and guided him inside her, lowering herself onto his cock, gasping slightly as she did so.

"Mrs. Marcus seems nice," she said.

Lee moved his hips, finding her rhythm and matching it. "I don't want to think about her right now."

"And her daughters too. They seem... nice."

"If you say so."

"I do. I like it here."

Lee grabbed two handfuls of her ass. He was barely listening. He glanced over at the lone painting in the room, which depicted four nude men being whipped by a skeleton while fire danced around them, and looked away.

"We should stay awhile," said Anya.

"Sure."

Something splashed onto his chest. He tore his eyes away from Anya's perfect form and looked down at the red splotch on his chest.

"Hey," he said, "what's that?"

"They all seem so... *nice.*"

"An, I'm serious. Are you—"

She was.

Blood poured from her nose.

"Hey, stop!"

But she didn't. She ground her pelvis against him.

"You're bleeding all over me!"

"Don't... stop..."

He shoved her backwards, and she fell, tumbling off him and almost taking his dick with her. She looked at him as if she had no idea where she was.

"Why did you—"

She touched her hand to her nose, and it came away bright red.

"Oh god," she said.

"I know," said Lee. "I was trying to tell you."

She shuffled off the bed and ran through to the bathroom. He heard the water splashing in the basin.

"You okay?" he shouted.

"I'm fine," came her muffled response.

He adjusted his position until he was able to see her through the door, reflected in the bathroom mirror. She gazed at herself, not doing anything to stop the blood flow. It ran down her face, her chin, dribbling onto her breasts. He worried she was having an aneurysm, and went to her. As he approached, she saw him.

"No!" she screamed, and slammed the door. He barged it open in time to see her punching her fist into the mirror. It shattered, long shards dropping into the basin.

"What the hell did you do that for?" said Lee.

She briefly glanced at him, then her gaze returned to the mirror. She peered into it as if seeking some hidden meaning.

"I saw something," she said.

He put his hand on her shoulder and she recoiled. "Don't touch me!"

He withdrew, holding up both hands. "Hey, it's okay. It's all right."

A piece of glass dropped from the frame, landing alongside the others. Anya looked at him. Something burned behind her eyes, but not like when they were fucking. This was different.

"I'm sorry," she said. "I don't know what happened."

She glanced at the broken mirror, and when she looked back at him, she seemed normal again.

"You scared me," said Lee. He ran some toilet paper under the faucet and dabbed at her face, cleaning the blood away. When they were finished, he put his hand on the small of her back and guided her gently back to the bed. As he did so, the door opened.

"Would you look at these fucking clothes," said Garrett as he stormed in, only shutting up when he spotted Lee and Anya standing naked by the bed.

Anya squealed and tried to cover herself, running back into the bathroom and giving Garrett an unobstructed view of her ass. Lee didn't bother trying to hide.

"That's the second time you've seen my dick today. I'm beginning to think it's deliberate."

Garrett laughed. "Oh Toilet, it's not my fault you can't keep your goddam pants on. What were you doing, thinking of those chicks?"

"Actually—"

"That's all I've been doing. Damn, you see the way they were looking at Peter? Bet he's banging one of 'em right now, that lucky bastard."

"You here for a reason?" said Lee.

"Yeah, wanted to show you my new look," he said, spinning on the spot. He wore a too-tight white polyester suit that looked like it had been in storage since the 1970s.

"Nice," grinned Lee. "But doesn't John Travolta want his suit back?"

"Looks better on me," said Garrett. "What'd they give you to wear? You should see Lucy. Actually, wait, I'll go get her."

With that, he scurried off, and Anya poked her head round the door. "Is he gone?"

"Yeah, but he's coming back," said Lee, as he hurriedly slipped on a robe.

"He saw me *naked,* Lee. Do your friends not knock?"

"My *friends* do," he said absently. "Garrett doesn't."

Footsteps pounded along the hall, and Anya ducked back into the bathroom as Garrett reappeared in the room with Lucy, who was dressed like a 1920s flapper girl in a knee-length patterned dress.

"Would you look at her?" said Garrett. "She's like some old bitch from a black-and-white movie, don't ya think?"

"I think I look good," said Lucy. "It fits nice."

"You look better than fucking *Scarface* over there," said Lee, pointing to Garrett.

"Hey, say hello to my leeeeeeettle friend," sneered Garrett in the world's worst Al Pacino impersonation.

From downstairs a bell sounded.

"Supper time!" grinned Garrett. "Come on, quit standing around yakking and get dressed. Papa's hungry!" He grabbed Lucy and shoved his face into her chest as he said it, and she fought him off with the weariness of someone who's spent two decades living with Garrett. Lee couldn't help feeling a little sorry for her.

"Seriously though," said Garrett, "Let's go. I'm hungry."

"I'll join you as soon as you fuck off and let me get

dressed," said Lee. "And Garrett, make sure you wrap up warm. Wouldn't want you to come down with a Saturday Night Fever."

Garrett flipped him the bird and left with Lucy in tow, and then all was quiet once more.

10

Lee and Anya made their way downstairs, arm-in-arm. They had left Anya a blue dress with bows and ruffles, almost as old-fashioned as Lucy's outfit. Lee, on the other hand, looked like a Canadian logger in denim jeans and a plaid shirt with worn elbows and tattered sleeves. As a couple, they looked ridiculous, so Lee figured they would fit in nicely with the others. He looked forward to seeing what Peter was wearing. A sailor suit? Army fatigues? Full scuba gear?

"You ready?" he said, pausing in front of the dining-room door.

"As ready as I'll ever be," said Anya.

She pushed the door open. An enormous mahogany table greeted them, large enough to seat at least twenty people. At the head of the table was Mrs. Marcus, with Bethany to her right and Patricia to her left. Next to Bethany sat Garrett and Lucy. There were three more settings laid out.

"Good evening," said Mrs. Marcus. "Please, do sit down."

They took their seats opposite Garrett and Lucy.

"Where's Peter?" said Lee.

"Your friend will not be joining us this evening," said Mrs. Marcus.

"He has a stomach ache," said Bethany. Lee thought he caught a sly glance between Bethany and her mom.

"Well," said Garrett, looking absurd in his white disco suit, "then there's no one to wait for. Let's eat!" He reached out across the table for a sizzling chicken leg, and Bethany slapped his wrist.

"We're still waiting on our sister," she said primly.

"Your sister?"

"There are more of you?" said Lucy.

"Oh yes," said Mrs. Marcus. "We cannot start without my eldest daughter at the table. But don't worry... here she is now." The old lady smiled and looked to the back of the room.

"Good evening, Jenifer," she said.

The name alone wasn't enough to interest Garrett. He had, indeed, forgotten the girl was ever called Jenifer.

It had all been so long ago. He couldn't remember what he'd eaten for breakfast that morning, never mind the name of a girl he had known for one evening.

But when he turned and saw her face, it all came back to him. His stomach flipped. The delicious smell of hot food made him nauseous. He turned to Lucy, and he saw it in her eyes too.

The recognition.

But it was impossible. Absolutely impossible, for reasons that were better left buried.

Like Jenifer is.

She stood like a specter, as beautiful as he remembered, as beautiful as she was that rainy night twenty years ago, hitchhiking on a lonely forest road, picked up by a van full of kids in their early twenties, kids who were drunk and high and looking for a good time, whatever the cost.

"Good evening, mother," she said. She looked at the new faces, seeming to linger on Garrett.

You're imagining it. She's dead. The bitch is dead.

"It's so nice to see new faces." She walked lightly, as if carried on the breeze, wearing a white blouse and skirt, the same ones she had been wearing—

No! It wasn't possible!

Even if she had somehow survived and dug her way out of the shallow grave, she would be in her late thirties now. The girl who took a seat next to Lee could be no older than eighteen.

Her daughter?

Yeah, nice one, genius. She gave birth after she died?

Okay, then. Her twin.

That makes even less sense.

"Garrett?" hissed Lucy, and he stared blankly at her. "Jenifer asked your name."

He turned to the girl, his throat dry. "It's—"

"Garrett," she finished for him. "Yes, I know."

"How day you know my name?" he said.

"Because I just told her," said Lucy through clenched teeth.

"Are you okay?" asked Jenifer. "Can I get you something? Some water? Or a bottle of wine?"

He felt hot, too hot, and worked to loosen his shirt collar. "No, no bottle. I mean, no wine. I mean—"

"What *do* you mean?" said Jenifer.

"I mean, yes. Some wine, please. No bottle."

The bottle. He remembered what he had done with the bottle.

"My dear," said Mrs. Marcus. "Please sit down and let our guests enjoy their meal. I'm sure they didn't expect the third degree."

Jenifer smiled at her mom and took a seat. "Shall we say grace?"

"No," said Mrs. Marcus. "I don't think that will be necessary tonight."

Garrett stole a quick look at Lucy. She glared at him and shook her head almost imperceptibly.

Patricia stood and leaned across the table, ladling the soup into bowls as Bethany handed them to the diners. Garrett looked anywhere but at Jenifer.

It's not her. It can't be her. You're being a douche.

"This soup is delicious," said Lee. "What's your secret?"

Mrs. Marcus looked both proud and embarrassed. "Oh, a little of this and a little of that. My secret recipe, if you'll indulge me." Then, to seemingly no one in particular, she said, "Why thank you, dear. That's most kind."

Did Lee recognize her? He should. He was there, for part of it at least. Wasn't he? It was hard to recall the events of that night accurately. There had been so much alcohol, so many drugs. Pills, coke, uppers, downers... the evening had been a blur, and now, with the passing of so many years, it barely qualified as a memory. More of a dream.

Or a nightmare.

"Don't you like your soup?" asked Patricia.

"Who, me?" said Garrett. His appetite had abandoned him. He lifted the spoon and sipped for the benefit of his hosts. "Mmmm," he said. "Tasty."

"After supper, we thought we could play some games," said Bethany.

"You like games?" said Jenifer.

Garrett couldn't speak. Luckily, Lucy did.

"I think we'll go straight to bed. It's been a long day, and we wouldn't want to put you to any more trouble."

"Oh nonsense!" bubbled Patricia. "We do love to play games. It gets so boring, just the three of us."

"The *four,* my dear," said Mrs. Marcus.

"Oh yes, how silly of me."

Garrett could have sworn they exchanged a knowing glance.

"Play with us," said Bethany, and Garrett had a vague flashback to a scary film he had seen once, where some writer had been trapped in a haunted hotel. The allusion was not one he relished.

"So tomorrow morning, you'll drive us into town?" said Lee. "My car's at a garage not too far from here. If you just—"

"We can discuss that in the morning," said Mrs. Marcus. "For now, eat up, and then you children can play your game."

"Not me," said Jenifer. "I'm tired. All of this excitement has taken its toll."

Garrett breathed a sigh of relief. He couldn't take much more of this. He felt himself wilting under Jenifer's gaze. He was sure she was staring at him, though he didn't dare look at her to confirm his suspicions.

"Where were you going, anyway?" asked Bethany.

"We rented a cabin up the mountain," said Lucy.

Lee looked at her. "I thought you said you guys owned it?"

Garrett winced internally. "Yeah, well, we lied." He stared into his soup. "Things haven't been going so great for us recently."

"Hey man, I'm sorry to hear that," said Lee.

"Yeah, well, it is what it is. We rented the van as well, so now we're really fucked." He gave Mrs. Marcus an apologetic look. "Sorry about the language, ma'am."

Something crashed next door. It sounded like pots and pans falling to the floor. In an instant, Mrs. Marcus was on her feet, so fast that her chair toppled backwards.

"Excuse me," she said, "But I must see to that."

"Is someone else here?" said Lucy.

"No," answered Bethany. "It's just us. Isn't that right, Patricia?"

"Yes. There's no one here but us."

"Maybe it's Peter?" said Lee.

"Oh, I don't think so," giggled Bethany. She slurped her soup. "I really don't think so."

Mrs. Marcus never returned, and soon supper was finished. As Jenifer retired to her room and the Patricia and Bethany cleared the table, Lee, Anya, Garrett, and Lucy found themselves ushered into a large and near-empty games room.

"You okay, man?" Lee asked Garrett. He thought he would have been thrilled to hear about Garrett's money woes, and yet revelry was conspicuous by its absence. "Look, if you're short of cash, I can—"

"No," he replied. "It's not that bad."

"Not that bad?" sneered Lucy. She had taken up residence by the window, leaning her head out and smoking from a rapidly dwindling carton. "We're three months late with our mortgage."

"We'll make it up," he said, visibly uncomfortable

discussing it in front of Lee. "I wonder what games they want to play?"

He was trying to change the subject, and Lee let him.

"Dunno, but if it's a dance-off, you're sure to win in that suit," he said, trying to lighten the mood. Garrett glanced nervously towards the door, then turned conspiratorially to Lee.

"You recognize her?" he said.

"Who?"

Garrett's voice dropped to a whisper. "The third sister. Jenifer."

"I don't think so. Why?"

"I—"

"Shut up, Garrett," said Lucy. Thin smoke wafted from her cigarette. "It can't be her."

"What are you talking about?" said Anya.

"It looks exactly like her," Garrett said to Lucy. "And you know it."

"Yes, but it's *not*. It's a coincidence, that's all. Don't be a moron."

Garrett's eyes shifted to Lee. "You remember that trip we took after graduation?"

Lee nodded.

"I told you to drop it," said Lucy.

"It's her," he said. "Fuck, it even *sounds* like her."

"And you'd know better than anyone," she said.

"Would someone tell me what's going on?" said Anya. Lee didn't want to tell her. And why should he? Garrett was being delusional. Sure, Jenifer resembled the girl... but he couldn't recall her voice or her face with that level of clarity. He had barely met her.

Garrett stared at Lucy. "I'm telling you, it's—"

"It's what?" said Lucy. "It's her, back from the grave to haunt us by making us soup and going to bed?"

The door opened. Patricia and Bethany entered, each balancing a tray of drinks.

"We hope you enjoyed supper," said Bethany.

"And now we can play a game," said Patricia.

It struck Lee for the first time how much of a double act they were, as if the whole routine had been rehearsed. He pictured Statler and Waldorf from *The Muppets,* and almost burst out laughing.

"What do you have in mind?" he said, clenching his jaw to keep his composure.

"Spin The Bottle," said Bethany, and this time Lee did laugh. He couldn't help it.

"Sorry," he said. "I'm forty-two years old. I'm not playing a children's game."

Patricia fixed him with a stare.

"You're never too old to play," she said.

Anya's fingers entwined Lee's. "Yeah, not tonight," she said. "We're going to bed. It's been a long day."

"A pity," said Bethany. She looked at her sister and laughed.

Lee could still hear them laughing as he and Anya left the room and headed for the stairs.

GARRETT WATCHED AS LUCY CRUSHED HER CIGARETTE BUTT between her fingers. "Look," she said, "Thank you for taking us in for the night. I really mean that. But seriously, we're not little kids anymore. We don't play games."

"We used to," said Garrett. "We used to be fun. Or have you forgotten?"

She snorted out a derisive laugh. "That's the problem with you, Garrett. Things moved on. Everyone we knew moved on and left us behind. Now all we've got is the good old days, the memories, the yearbook. We were the prom king and queen... and so what? No one cares anymore. We're nothing. We're *shit.*"

"*You're* shit," he replied. It was not a great comeback.

"Yeah, good one," she said.

All the while the two girls watched in silence, vapid smiles fixed to their faces.

"You know, it's all your fault," said Garrett.

"Oh yeah?" said Lucy.

"Yeah. You held me back. I could have been somebody, but oh no, you wanted to get a house, a job, a kid, and—"

A kid.

He tried to stop himself, but it was too late. The next thing he knew she was standing before him, and his cheek stung from her slap.

"You bastard," she said. "You rotten bastard. You ruined your *own* life. I just wish you hadn't ruined mine too."

He rubbed at his cheek.

"When we get home, I'm leaving," said Lucy. "I should have left you that night twenty—"

He struck her with his fist, hard enough to send her stumbling backwards. She stared at him, shocked, and he moved to hit her again.

"That was how it started, wasn't it?" said Lucy. "You hit her because she wouldn't—"

"Get out!" he roared. "Get the fuck out of my face! That bitch had it coming, and if you don't fuck off, I'll..."

"You'll what? You'll rape me too? You'll kill me and bury me in the woods? Go for it. But bury me deep, you motherfucker. Bury me deep or I'll come back. I swear to Christ in heaven, I'll come back for you."

He took a deep breath, and said, "You're not so innocent."

They stared at each other for a long time, Lucy watching him through wet, haunted eyes, a purple bruise forming on her cheek.

"You bastard," she said, and then she turned and walked calmly past the two girls and left the room.

Bethany turned to Garrett.

"Is she not playing, then?"

～

Lucy stepped into the hallway and blinked away tears.

That asshole.

He blamed her for everything, she knew that. It was why he sought solace in the arms — and between the legs — of other women. He didn't even try to hide it anymore. And yet she stood by him, always had, even when she had left him alone with the baby, and he had drunk too much, and fallen asleep, and... and...

It'll all be okay.

She laughed dryly. He had done it again, gotten in her head, the way he always did whenever she threatened to leave.

What'll you do without me? He would say. *You need me as much as I need you.*

Gaslighting bastard. She wouldn't fall for it, not this time.

You always tell yourself that.

But this time she *meant* it.

Garrett's upset. He didn't mean what he said. That girl, that Jenifer...

What about her? She was dead. Fucking *dead*. They had killed her, Garrett and his friends. And so what if she wasn't? Say it *was* her ghost seeking revenge... what business would Jenifer have with her? She played no part in that ghastly night. There was no blood on *her* hands.

"Good evening, Lucy."

The voice came from all around. Lucy looked for the source, for Jenifer.

"Where are you?" she said.

"Are you not playing with my sisters?"

Lucy scanned the darkness that lurked beyond the flame of the candles. She couldn't see anyone.

"I think they want to play with my boyfriend," she said.

"I thought you liked to watch?"

Suddenly Lucy was afraid. She took a step back, her hand groping for the door handle. Unable to locate it, she turned.

The door was gone. In its place was a blank, endless wall. She ran her hands over it, searching, but found nothing. A cold breeze drifted by, carrying with it the charnel smell of spoiled meat. Something brushed her back and she screamed, but when she spun on her heels there was nothing there. She was in a featureless corridor, lit by a seemingly infinite procession of candles.

Lucy's heart pounded.

She tried to speak but no words came out.

"You do *like to watch, don't you?"*

She turned in the direction of the voice, squinting down the corridor. There, at the very end, was an open door, a figure standing in it, dressed in white.

"You're dead," said Lucy, surprised how easily she abandoned her rational mind. "They killed you."

The figure moved a step closer, the candles next to her extinguishing, the door behind her disappearing into obsidian blackness.

"I know."

She stepped forwards again as another set of candles snuffed out.

Lucy tottered backwards on her heels. She kicked them off. The noise of them clattering to the floor was outrageously loud.

"I didn't do anything," she said in a small voice.

A third set of lights went out.

"I know. You just watched, didn't you?"

"We were drunk," said Lucy. "We were stoned. I didn't know what was going on. I hardly even remember it." She was crying now, the wooden boards as cold as a tomb beneath her bare feet. She backed away as more lights went out, as if Jenifer wore the darkness itself as a shroud.

"I remember it well. I remember you, Lucy. I remember the way you laughed, the way you goaded them on."

"That's not true."

"Better me than you, right? Someone had to take one for the team?"

"That's not it. I... I just—"

"Do you still have the photos, Lucy?"

She sobbed, her legs trembling. "No," she said. "I burned them."

More lights extinguished. More, and more, getting faster, gaining on her.

Lucy turned and ran. Where, she didn't know. There was only one way to go. No doors, no rooms, no passageways... just an impossible tunnel plunging into the encroaching darkness.

"Leave me alone!" she cried, breathless and panting, tears stinging her eyes. "I didn't do anything, I only..."

...watched as Garrett pulled the girl's hair, so hard a clump came out, the men all naked now, blood on their penises, the flash from the Polaroid briefly lighting the room, a glimpse of banal reality, Lucy laughing as the girl begged for her life, the girl who earlier had been flirting with Garrett, or maybe just talking to him, and Lucy...

...knew that Jenifer was close to her now, the darkness creeping up on her like a dark cancer spreading through the veins of the diseased house, this house of madness, of *horror*.

She daren't turn, lest the glimpse of Jenifer's face drive her insane. Ahead she could see the vague outline of a door. She balled her fists and lowered her head, feet pounding as fast as her heart. She had to reach the door.

It was her only chance.

PART III

The Great Fatso

12

Lee lay in bed watching Anya grapple with the bows and frills of her dress, trying to lift it over her head.

"I don't know how they managed to get undressed back then," she said.

"They had maids to help them."

He considered doing just that, but decided to watch her struggle instead. Their hosts had been gracious enough to supply them with clothes, but no underwear, and he was enjoying watching Anya's butt jiggle as she wrestled the outfit off. He hoped they could pick up where they left off before supper.

Before the incident with the mirror.

Soon she was free, the dress discarded by the bed. She quickly got under the covers, lying with her back to him. Lee lay facing her and placed his hand on her waist.

"Lee, stop." Her voice had lost the playful tone of earlier. "I'm tired."

"Just getting comfortable," he said, wrapping his arm fully around her, cupping one breast, toying gently with her nipple.

"I said stop. Please."

He kissed the back of her neck, pulling her towards him.

A nightmarish shriek echoed throughout the house.

Anya freed herself from his grasp and sat upright.

"What the fuck was that?"

"It sounded like a man," said Lee.

"Garrett?"

"I don't think so."

Anya was already getting out of bed. Icy blue moonlight streamed in through the window, highlighting her curves. The scream came again, louder this time, more desperate.

"Who *is* that?" said Anya.

"Who cares? Probably the old lady's husband."

"She said they live here alone." She fixed him with a stare. "I want to find out where that's coming from."

"I thought you were tired? It's none of our business."

She got out of bed. Two silk kimonos hung from a peg on the bathroom door. She slipped into one and tossed the other onto the bed.

"You coming with me or not?"

Lee sighed. "Fine. But I'm not wearing a fucking kimono."

He swung his legs over the edge of the bed and tugged the borrowed jeans back over his hips, zipping them up extra carefully the way a man must when he's not wearing underwear.

He felt Anya's hand on his arm. She offered him a candle, and he took it.

"This is ridiculous, you know that?"

"Humor me," she said.

❧

"Guess we can't play with only three of us," said Garrett.

He kneeled on the hardwood floor, Bethany and Patricia sitting cross-legged in front of him, an empty wine bottle between them.

"Of course we can," said Bethany.

"It's more fun this way," said Patricia. "The loser has to sit and watch."

"Well, I guess that makes me the winner whichever way you slice it," he grinned.

Patricia blushed. "You want to spin the bottle?"

"Sure, I'll do the honors." He looked at their eager faces, and wondered if he would be their first. "Don't get many men round here, I guess?"

"Oh, you'd be surprised," said Bethany.

"She's joking," said Patricia. She looked at her hands clasped on her lap. "I've never even *kissed* a boy."

"Me neither," said Bethany.

Garrett's grin grew wider. "Well, that's just about the saddest story I ever heard."

"It's okay," said Patricia. "We practise on each other."

As she said it, Garrett was throwing back one of the shots from the tray. He choked, the liquid streaming out of his nostrils.

"You, uh, what?"

"We practise on each other," said Bethany. She looked at her sister. "I think we've gotten quite good at it."

"It was weird at first," said Patricia.

"What, kissing your sister?"

"No," she said, her face stony. "The first time she fucked me."

Garrett just stared at them. The alcohol burned his throat. For once in his life, he was speechless.

"But it's not weird anymore," said Bethany. "Now, we really like it."

"Yes," said Patricia. "Now we fuck each other most nights."

Bethany smiled. "It's a good way to keep warm on those long winter nights. Don't you agree, Garrett?"

He nodded, his mind a total blank except for the image of the two girls—

"You going to spin the bottle?"

"Huh?" he wasn't even sure which one of them had said it. "Oh, yeah." He reached for the bottle, ashamed to see his hand shaking.

It whirred around, over and over, before landing on Bethany.

"Uh oh!" she squealed. "Guess I'm getting kissed!" Garrett moved towards her, and she held up a hand. "Wait, we've not spun it a second time."

"My turn," said Patricia. She took the bottle and whirled it around. It stopped abruptly, pointing directly at her.

"Oh, boo," she pouted, giving Garrett some side-eye.

"Don't sound too upset," said Bethany. The girl placed her hand on the back of her sister's neck and pulled her forwards. Their lips met, and then they were kissing. Garrett's heart rate increased. The girls pulled back slightly, a string of saliva the only thing keeping them together, and then their tongues were out, flicking each other. Bethany's hand found Patricia's breast, kneading it through the fabric of her dress, while Patricia reached for Bethany's zipper, pulling it down, exposing a triangle of pale, delicate flesh.

Uncharted territory, thought Garrett. *No-man's-land.*

Bethany shrugged the dress off her shoulders and it fell to her waist, her breasts bared, Patricia squeezing them. She turned to Garrett.

"Are you just going to sit there?" she said.

Lucy ran. She ran as fast as she could, her legs — which once upon a time had carried her to the status of head cheerleader — pumping furiously. Her feet ached, her ankles too.

Behind her, more lights went out, following her.

She could hear no footsteps except her own, but she knew the girl was right behind her.

Ahead of her was the door. Could she make it? Could she possibly outrun the dead?

Her breath came in sharp gasps.

Control your breathing. Control it!

But she couldn't.

Panic had taken ahold of her.

The screams had turned to low moans, like a dying animal caught in a trap.

Lee's candle shed little light on their surroundings. He could barely see Anya, and she was right next to him.

They came to a fork in the hallway, and waited, listening.

"It's coming from down there," said Anya, pointing to her right.

"Maybe we should leave it," said Lee. "It's probably a dog or something."

"That's no dog."

She swept past him and carried on down the hallway. Against his better judgement, Lee followed. Maybe if he indulged her curiosity, she would have sex with him again.

Christ, the lengths he would go for a few minutes of passion.

"Jesus," said Anya.

"What is it?"

Then he saw it. Shimmering into view was a door. Lee trembled.

"It can't be," he murmured.

There was a clown painted on the door. He leered over them, his face a grinning death mask, the paint dripping from his bulbous red nose. Anya ran a finger across it.

"Still wet," she said.

"The Great Fatso," said Lee. In the dim light he saw Anya staring at him, a look of confusion etched onto her face. He tried to explain. "My fifth birthday party. My mom hired a clown. The Great Fatso. He scared me so bad I hid in the bathroom." He swallowed hard. "Then, later, when I came out, he was waiting there. He—"

"Why are you telling me this?"

Lee cast his eyes over the grotesque image, freshly daubed on the door.

"Because that's him. That's The Great Fatso."

He looked into the clown's blank white eyes. The makeup was the same, almost skull-like, the white and black grease-paint matching the baggy checked trousers, held up by suspenders stretched tight over The Great Fatso's bulky shoulders. He held four red balloons that seemed to float all the way off the door, hovering in a strange dimension somewhere between the second and third.

Two of the balloons had been crossed out with sludgy black paint.

From behind the door came the most godawful wail either of them had ever heard.

"I can't go in there," said Lee.

"We have to. Someone could be hurt."

"But what if he's in there?"

"Who?"

Lee clenched his teeth. "The Great Fatso."

"It's not possible."

"Neither's eating supper with a dead girl."

Anya looked at him. "What did you say?"

And, with dreadful inevitability, that was the moment the door opened all by itself.

Garrett lay back, Bethany kneeling over him, kissing him with a strange and wonderful urgency. Patricia worked his belt buckle free, tugging his ridiculous white pants down over his legs. She grasped his penis, caressing it, and then he felt the warm sensation of her mouth on his cock.

Garrett reached blindly for Bethany's chest, the other hand finding the back of Patricia's head. Bethany pulled away from him. She stood and slipped her bunched-up dress off.

"You like what you see?" she said.

He nodded eagerly. It wasn't his first threesome — far from it — but it was his first with sisters. *Virgin* sisters, he reminded himself.

The *best* kind of sisters.

Lucy was almost at the door.

Thank god.

And what did she expect to find through there? Respite? Escape?

Maybe. Just *maybe*.

She couldn't run forever.

For the first time, she glanced over her shoulder, and there she was, Jenifer, *right there,* her face a battered and frightening horror, one eye hanging from its socket from when Peter had hit her with the shovel. She opened her mouth and dirt spilled out, grave dirt that swarmed with writhing maggots, her hands reaching, broken fingers clawing at the air, coming for her, and then Lucy was outside, outside the house, surrounded by trees and long grass and rain that poured down from the heavens, rain that never stopped, as if the sky itself was doomed to weep for eternity over this macabre nightmare.

She tripped, crashing to the ground, spinning onto her back and gazing up into the hellish face of...

Nothing.

There was nothing there, nothing but a rundown house with shattered windows, the lights off, vines and deep vegetation covering every square inch, mother nature claiming it as her own.

She was welcome to it.

"I beat you," she said, smiling an insane smile. "I fucking *beat* you."

Then the ground cracked beneath her, splitting wide, and Lucy fell deep into the bowels of the earth.

At least the door creaking open hid the ghoulish visage of Lee's childhood nightmare, The Great Fatso.

Yeah, small fucking mercies.

He and Anya shared a look. He held up his candle,

offering it to the darkness of the room. It took a moment for his eyes to adjust, and then he saw it.

The blood.

"Do you—"

"Yeah," she said. "I see it."

A large pool, spreading across the floor.

"Help me," said a voice, dark and tormented.

It's him, it's The Great Fatso.

Something glinted in the blood, a reflection.

"Who's there?" said Anya. She took a step forwards. One more, and she would officially cross the threshold. Lee put his arm out, halting her.

"What are you doing?" he said. He hardly recognized his own voice.

She didn't answer.

Instead, she pushed past Lee and entered the room.

Lucy hit the ground, sending shockwaves coursing through her body.

Forcing herself to move, she sat. Darkness enveloped her. She could have been floating through space were it not for the painful hardness of the ground beneath her.

"Why, Lucy?" said a voice in her ear. *"Of all of them, why you?"*

She broke down. "I'm sorry," she said.

"Yes. That's what they all say. That they're so very, very sorry."

"But I *am!*"

"You are now, yes. Now that your actions have consequences, and not a second before."

She looked around, but could see no one.

Whick.

A match...

...struck, the Polaroids nestled in the bottom of a steel waste-paper basket, images depicting the slow and maddeningly casual degradation and destruction of a young woman who's only crime was to ask for help from a group of strangers, young people like herself, college students on a road trip, college students who posed with her as they fucked her, who laughed, who poured alcohol on her screaming naked body and...

...the hem of Lucy's flapper girl dress caught fire, sparking instantly, erupting into flame.

"No!" she cried, kicking her legs, desperately trying to disrobe. But the fire spread quickly. Her skin sizzled, coming up in blisters that popped and disgorged their acrid, stinking contents over her legs, the patterned fabric sticking to her, becoming part of her flesh. The shoulder strap was next, heating up, burning, boiling, bursting into flame. It licked at her face, the fire rising, the scent of burning hair and meat catching in her nostrils, choking her, her skin melting, the...

...corners of the photographs curling, the images blackening, obscuring the laughing, drunken faces, burning, burning, until no trace remained...

...and then nothing but emptiness, a void as one more soul was snuffed out like so many useless candles.

Garrett couldn't hear much, what with Bethany's thighs clamped over his ears. He felt her blood pulsing through her veins, while Patricia worked his penis. There was no way this girl hadn't done it before. She was too good, too perfect, but he didn't care. It was a dumb thing to think about.

His ankles tightened, like a boa constrictor had wrapped itself around them.

"Jesus," he tried to say, but Bethany's pussy pressed against his face, preventing him. He reached for her, hands groping wildly, shoving her, pushing her off him as warm liquid poured over his face, gushing from her vagina like a faucet. It filled his mouth instantly, spilling over the sides, and he knew it was blood.

Bethany finally released him and stood, blood still splattering from between her legs. Garrett covered his face, wiping the crimson liquid away. He looked down to see Mrs. Marcus staring up at him with her wrinkled lips over his cock. Her dentures rested on his stomach, and she grinned up at him.

Garrett spat out the coppery-tasting blood, and screamed, *"What the fuck?"*

"Miss me?" said Bethany, only it wasn't her, not anymore.

It was Jenifer.

He turned to her, and she stood before him, the broken wine bottle jutting out from her vagina, filling with blood that sloshed around inside as she strode towards him. She reached down and gripped the bottle by the neck, wrenching it free and unleashing a torrent of gore over Garrett, the blood...

...drumming steadily off the floor as he stepped back, the bottle sticking out between her legs, her motionless legs, a brooding silence descending, no one sure what to say, no one sure what to do, unable to even look at each other, the party over, the girl dead, her...

...smile as she kneeled by Garrett, his arms pinned by Bethany and Patricia, their mother dribbling saliva over his now-limp cock.

She held the bottle to his face.

"Remember this?" she said.

He did.

He could never forget it.

~

Lee's candle flickered. He cupped a hand over it.

"Anya?"

"I'm right here."

He couldn't see her, his heart thumping an irregular beat. Somewhere nearby, pipes groaned, the floorboards creaking underfoot. With every step he expected The Great Fatso to come lumbering from the shadows like he had that day, his enormous baggy clown pants at his ankles.

Come sit on my lap, birthday boy.

"You see anything?" he said, trying to push the perverted funnyman from his thoughts.

"Quiet," said Anya. "Do you hear that?"

Lee listened. "No. What is it?"

A moment of silence, and then she said, "I hear something breathing."

Some*thing*. Not some*one*.

He heard it too. Shallow, rasping breaths, and then the clanking of heavy chains scraping along the floor.

"Let's get out of here," he said.

No reply.

"Anya?"

"I'm here."

He squinted into the darkness, searching for the light from her candle.

There.

He saw it, oddly far away. How big was this room? He took a step closer.

"Don't move, I see you."

Treading carefully, he followed the glow. It moved.

"Anya, I said stay put, I'm coming to you."

He was almost by her side now. So close. He longed to feel her touch, her closeness. The light from the candle was faint, illuminating nothing more than the hand that held it.

"Found you," he said, a smile crossing his face in the abominable darkness. He reached for her, found her arm.

"You sound so far away," she said.

Her voice was coming from behind him.

From the other side of the room.

Then who...

His fingers closed over the burly forearm. He raised his candle, past the oversized jacket with the flower on it, past the polka dot bowtie... he couldn't stop himself, his hand moving of its own free will.

"Anya!" he screamed, staggering backwards, hurling the candle against the floor and running, running until he hit someone, the pair of them collapsing to the ground, Lee screaming, Anya screaming, until they realized they were in each other's arms.

"What did you see?" said Anya breathlessly.

Lee clung to her, afraid to let her go. "It was him, he's come for me, he's come back to finish what he started."

"What are you talking about?"

"The Great Fatso! He's here!"

"Your birthday clown? Lee, get a grip!"

"I saw him! I—"

"Help me," came a weary voice.

Lee stood, hauling Anya to her feet, his head striking something hard, something made of glass...

A lightbulb.

He groped for it, finding a cord, pulling it, the intense

light of the bulb hurting his eyes. The first thing he did was look at Anya, make sure it was indeed her he was holding onto. It was. Their eyes met, and then as one they turned to the figure on the floor beside them.

The man stared back at them with rheumy, bloodshot eyes. His skin had been removed, ragged fragments of it framing his eyes and lips. The rest of his head was pulsing red tissue and muscle that dripped blood onto his once-white shirt.

A variety of weapons lay in front of him. Knives, hammers, wrenches, some stained with blood, others fresh and gleaming.

"Kill me," he said, the effort exhausting him. "Please, kill me."

"My god," said Lee. He pulled Anya closer. "Who did this to you?"

The man rattled out a husky breath. "Those women. They'll get you too."

"We have to leave," Lee said to Anya.

"I ain't going nowhere," said the skinless man. "I'm begging you... kill me. I shoulda been dead a long, long time ago."

Lee looked at Anya. "What do we do?"

She stared blankly back at him. "Do it."

"What?"

"Kill him. He's right."

"I can't do that..."

"Son," said the man. "Who are you talking to?"

A butcher knife whistled through the air, plunging into the man's neck. He threw his head back and wailed, as Anya brought the knife down, again and again, chopping off slices of muscle with each blow, the chunks of flesh dropping, some sticking to the blade. Blood sprayed uncontrollably from the wounds, drenching Anya. Lee watched in horrified, frozen silence.

She stabbed the man one final time, straight through the heart. He shuddered his dying breath. Only now did Lee notice the stink of piss and shit and blood. How long had this man been here? How many days, weeks, months...?

"What did you do to him?" He couldn't look at Anya. She had killed that man without a second thought.

"I had to do it," she said. "It was a mercy killing."

Dazed, he nodded, hardly listening. "We need to get out of here."

"What about the others?"

"Fuck them. They're probably long gone."

All around, bodies were piled floor-to-ceiling in various stages of decomposition, a doorway forming the only gap in the miserable slaughterhouse.

"What did you mean before?" asked Anya.

"Huh?"

"You said we ate dinner with a dead girl."

"I'll tell you once we're outside." He started past her, and suddenly the butcher knife pointed at his throat, the tip piercing his skin. "Jesus, what are you doing?"

"Tell me *now*."

What the fuck? Had she lost her mind? Well, she *had* just killed a man, so why not? She'd probably never be the same again. You can't kill someone and then go on living your life as normal.

"They killed her," he said. "Garrett and the others. I think. I wasn't there. I mean, I was at the cabin with them. We picked her up hitchhiking, brought her with us. I was dating Yuki Tagawa at the time. We went for a walk, took some acid. When we came back the next morning... the girl was gone. No one ever spoke about it, but I found..."

"You found what?"

He shrugged. "Evidence, I guess. Blood. A broken bottle. Lucy had some photos, but I only got a glimpse. I think they raped her, but I don't know. I swear to god, Anya, I wasn't there when it happened. She was at the cabin one day, and the next she wasn't. What was I supposed to do, go to the cops? By the time we left, everything had been cleaned up. It would be their word against mine."

"You fucking coward," she said. The blade pressed harder against his jugular.

"This isn't the time," he said.

"And that girl at supper..."

"That was her. I mean, it wasn't, obviously, but it looked like her, and I think it sounded like her. Jesus, An, it's been so long, I can't even remember myself. We were so *high*."

He realized he was close to tears. Anya lowered the knife, but didn't let go of it.

"I swear I wasn't there, Anya. I swear. Now let's go. Please."

"Okay," she said.

He was unsure if she believed him, but she should. He was telling the truth. They headed towards the door, Anya keeping a slight distance between them.

"Wait," said Lee. He stooped and picked up an axe from the floor. The edge was stained dark red, and he wondered how many of the bodies that surrounded them had been cut to pieces with the very weapon he clutched in his sweaty hands. Rejoining Anya by the door, he reached for the handle. As he opened the door, something niggled at the back of his mind, something the skinless man had said.

Son, who are you talking to?

13

THE DOOR OPENED.

"Jesus fucking Christ," said Lee.

The scene before them beggared belief, like a grisly tableau torn from his most feverish nightmares.

Garrett lay on his back, naked and prone, his ankles bound, wrists held above his head by Patricia and Bethany. Mrs. Marcus stood watching like a good mother should, arms crossed, nodding appreciatively.

And there, above Garrett, was Jenifer. She clutched a broken bottle in her hands, and she ground it into Garrett's crotch, twisting it, his penis visible through the green glass that rapidly filled with blood. He shrieked in agony, his voice ludicrously high-pitched, and Jenifer turned to the new arrivals and smiled.

"Welcome," she said, and then she popped the cork of the bottle with her thumb and great gouts of blood spewed from the neck like a fire hose.

Lee gripped the axe. It felt very heavy in his hands.

"Get him," said Mrs. Marcus, and Bethany rose, running towards him. Lee shoved Anya back, his girlfriend tripping and falling onto her ass as he raised the axe, swinging it in a wide arc at the approaching Bethany. It caught her in the neck, embedding itself, the metal striking bone. She fell, taking the axe with her, hands clutching frenziedly at her neck, blood bubbling from the gaping wound. Lee stepped on her stomach and pulled the axe free. He saw Patricia coming for him.

"Lee, no!" shouted Anya.

He ignored her, slamming the handle of the axe into Patricia's face. Her nose exploded and she staggered back, but Lee wasn't done. He smacked the weapon into her chest. She fell, and he brought the weapon screaming down again. The girl rolled, but not fast enough. The axe severed her arm with one clean cut. She looked up at him with a mouthful of blood, clutching at the stump of bone protruding from her shoulder.

Bethany clawed at his legs. Somehow the bitch wasn't dead yet. He kicked her onto her back, aiming the axe at what remained of her neck. The blade smacked hard off the floor, her severed head tumbling across the boards and coming to rest by the wall.

Her eyes were still open, and Lee moved in for one final blow. When she started to laugh, he stopped dead.

"You can't get away," said Bethany's head.

"But I didn't do anything!" he roared. Was he going mad? Or had he already lost his mind the moment he set foot in this cursed place, this hell? He cast his eyes at Garrett, who shuddered as Jenifer twisted the bottle. Without Bethany or Patricia to restrain him, he sat, reaching for Jenifer.

She dug the bottle in harder, using it in a scooping motion, and Garrett fell back again, howling. The dead girl lifted the bottle, turning it over and emptying its contents on

Garrett's stomach. Along with the expected blood, something limp and meaty plopped out.

That was enough for Lee. He threw the axe to the ground, grabbed Anya by the hand, and pulled her to her feet.

"Come on!" he said, dragging her behind him, leaping over Bethany's fidgeting torso, the girl's laugh echoing after them.

"Lee, wait," said Anya, but he couldn't. What was she thinking? She tried to shake free.

"What are you doing?" said Lee.

"Let me go," she said. She still held the knife in her other hand, and she thrust it towards him. It entered his belly. Somehow, it wasn't as painful as he would have expected. He looked down at the knife sticking out of him.

"Why?"

She withdrew the blade, ready to attack again. Lee balled a fist and punched her in the face. She hit the ground, dropping the knife. He looked through the doorway and there was Jenifer, front and center, coming for him. Patricia too, blood pumping from her shoulder and chest. Behind them, Bethany's decapitated torso crawled across the floor, hands searching for her head. Mrs. Marcus just laughed.

It was a fucking madhouse.

He turned his back on them, running, holding a hand to his bleeding stomach. He descended the stairs three at a time, trying not to trip, for to fall would surely mean certain death. Over his shoulder he saw them coming, the mutant freakshow of women following him down the stairs.

"I didn't do anything! I wasn't even there!"

The stairs kept going, down and down, the walls closing

in on him. Something bounded down the stairs, rolling past him.

Bethany's head. She was still laughing at him.

"Leave me alone!" he screamed, as if anyone could hear him.

What about Anya?

She had turned on him. She was lost, lost to the madness of the house. But when had it happened? When she had killed that man? Or earlier, the moment they had arrived?

The stairs finally ended, and Lee ran for the door ahead of him. The way out?

Who fucking knows?

He hit it with his shoulder, the door bursting open. A huge room greeted him, lined with dozens — no, hundreds — of beds, like a military hospital. He took a tentative step inside, closing the door behind him, locking it with the bolt.

The beds weren't empty.

Figures lay in each of them, the white sheets drawn up over their faces.

Lee walked forwards, his bare feet scuffing along the floor, afraid to make a sound. He heard footsteps on the stairs. They were nearly here. He had locked the door, but what good would that do against psychotic undead women?

A fist pounded against the door, and all at once the bodies in the beds sat up, their faces still hidden by the sheets. Lee spun, looking at the strange faceless figures, hundreds of them, their heads slowly turning towards him.

"I didn't do anything," he said uselessly.

The door opened behind him. The figures pulled the sheets from their faces and left their beds. Women, all women, hundreds of them, stalking naked towards him with vacant expressions on their faces.

"I wasn't even there," he said, sinking to his knees as the women advanced. "I didn't do anything..."

He felt a hand on his shoulder.

"Lee," said Anya.

"Why?" he sobbed.

"I saw what you did. Mrs. Marcus opened my eyes. She showed me in the bathroom mirror. At first I didn't believe it. It wasn't the sort of thing you'd do. You're one of the nice guys, aren't you?"

"I am."

"But you do get angry sometimes, don't you?"

"I didn't even *touch* her," he said. "I was with my ex-girlfriend the whole time."

"And then I started thinking... why were your friends being so mean to me? Why were they ignoring me? Why didn't they even say hello, or answer my questions?"

He shook his head. He didn't understand.

The women formed a circle around them.

Anya moved closer, her face inches from his.

"I didn't remember either, not until the mirror," she said, and then Lee closed his...

...eyes were shut, she was asleep, fast asleep, it had been a busy day and she was tired, but when Lee came home he was drunk, and he got into bed, horny like he always got after a few drinks, and though she tried to fight him off he was too strong, too belligerent, and he fucked her, against her will, in their own bed, tearing her panties off and forcing his way inside of her, hurting her, hurting her so bad that she screamed and hit him, she hit him and scratched his face and he got mad then, real mad, his face screwing up, and he punched her, once, twice, over and over, his hands closing over her throat, choking her, her vision blurring, the light fading, and then... and then nothing.

Just nothing but the infinite emptiness of death.

"You killed me, Lee," she said. She smiled. "I've been dead for a week, and I didn't even know it."

"It's not possible," he said, his head spinning. "It's fucking insane. You're all insane! All of you! All—"

Then the women descended upon him.

They grabbed his hands, pulling his fingers until his knuckles cracked and the digits were torn off and discarded. His hands were next, the skin tearing, blood splattering noisily across the floor as the women snapped his wrists, twisted them back and forth until the bones ground to dust. Some of the women took his legs, pulling them apart like a wishbone, his pants ripping up the seams, his legs tearing from his body as the pressure built in his groin.

"I'm sorry!" he screamed, and the women laughed at that.

Poor men.

They were *always* sorry.

14

ANYA LIKED IT HERE.

The women were so accommodating. Nothing was too much trouble for them. On the first night, they had shown her to her own bed, beside her new friends Patricia and Bethany, and then the next morning, after a long and dreamless sleep, Mrs. Marcus had invited her to a private breakfast. Anya ate until her stomach was fit to burst, listening as Mrs. Marcus explained about her house for wronged women. She gave Anya a choice, and Anya accepted her offer.

That evening, the women were summoned, and deep in the underground chamber, Mrs. Marcus performed the ritual granting Anya eternal vengeance.

"May I call you mom?" asked Anya afterwards, and Mrs. Marcus smiled and said yes, she could. Then she went upstairs to the mysterious room, the one that was different inside depending on who opened the door, and paid the occupant a visit.

She thought it amusing that she still lived with her ex-boyfriend. Oh sure, he had a roommate, a funny old clown who spoke only in grunts and seemed to be a terrible sexual degenerate, but she thought she'd check on him every so often to make sure he was okay. He couldn't go anywhere, what with having no arms or legs, but she wanted to check he was still in as much pain as ever. And if he wasn't, she made sure to cut him a few times.

He wouldn't live forever, Mrs. Marcus had told her, but he could last a long time if properly cared for. He was like a house plant who needed fed and watered every so often, and that was good.

Because Anya had always enjoyed her house plants.

In fact, she prided herself on keeping them alive for a long, long time.

AFTERWORD

Horror House of Perversion was written as a screenplay in 1975.

It was borne of a chance meeting with none other than the King of Exploitation movies himself, Roger fuckin' Corman. And where did this illustrious meeting take place? Why, where else but the lingerie department of Sears?

I remember it well, because my girlfriend at the time had handed me some underwear to hold, and when I saw Roger passing by, I called his name and waved a pair of little blue panties at him.

He smiled at me and stopped to talk for a moment, no doubt terrified by the bearded fucking hippie with the handful of ladies' undergarments. I told him I was a screen-writer, and could I show him some of my work. He was a gentleman, and asked for the titles, because in those days, the quality of the film didn't matter as long as you had a shit-hot title and poster.

This was it, my big chance to impress Roger Corman... and my mind went blank. I forgot the name of every stupid script I had ever written — the ones I had lying around my house, the one I had just finished, the one I was working on, the one that had almost been made by Universal until they decided to steal my story and release it under a different name without giving me credit...

I stood there, red-faced and blustering, watching as Roger glanced at his watch, looking around for someone to save him from the panty-wielding lunatic.

Then it came to me.

"Horror House of Perversion," I said.

He nodded thoughtfully. "I like it," he said. "Send me the script."

I figured he was trying to politely get the fuck away from me, and I couldn't blame him. He said goodbye, and I wandered out of the store in a daze, grinning like an asshole until the mall cop knocked me to the ground in front of everyone and tried to arrest me for stealing women's underwear, which were — of course — still clutched in my hand.

For many years I had the local newspaper from the following day, with the headline LOCAL PERVERT WRITER STEALS PANTIES, framed on my office wall.

I never did hear back from Roger, and it wasn't until about a decade later that I bumped into my now ex-girlfriend, and she told me she'd been pissed off at me that day because I'd forgotten to buy eggs or something, so when I'd asked her to post my script, she'd actually posted a copy of the local newspaper with my face splashed on the front cover.

Well, *shit*. What ya gonna do, friend?

ALSO BY CARL JOHN LEE

The Blood Beast Mutations

"A horrific creature-feature splatterfest. Lee has created a high-speed chase of a story."

Steve Stred, author of RITUAL *and* WAGON BUDDY

"The Blood Beast Mutations is a highly entertaining story. It starts somewhere recognisable, and then slowly adds fear, then horror into the narrative. It's a fast-paced read that doesn't sacrifice story for thrills."

Mark Green, Reel Horror Show

ABOUT THE AUTHOR

A New York-based screenwriter, Carl John Lee has written a bunch of movies you've either never seen, or would never admit to seeing.

He wrote his debut novella, The Blood Beast Mutations, in 2020, disgusted and horrified by the world around him.

Inspired by Roger Corman and the golden age of exploitation films, Lee probes deep into the filthy underbelly of America, contrasting his bleak worldview with dark humour.

Made in United States
North Haven, CT
01 July 2022

20835434R00071